SPORT STORY

VOLUME 1

Superstar Coach

For all the players still practicing after everyone
else has gone home.

Also by Thomas Taylor

Sport Story®

Contents

Superstar Coach

CHAPTER I
The Players

All the other kids had gone home already. It was just Jimmy and the basket. He could imagine all the moves the pros make and then try to copy them. He could practice his left-handed dribble, his jump shots, and even try to dunk. He was all by himself and Jimmy liked it this way best. Sometimes Jimmy would stay two or three hours after everyone else had left. He loved the game of basketball and knew that through hard work and dedicated practice, he could one day make the NBA. He had convinced himself of that.

It was not just the game of basketball that kept Jimmy there after everyone else had left. It was also the fact that he had no one to go home to. His mother worked the late shift at the hospital and his father had died when he was only a little boy. Except for caddying part-time at the country club golf course, all Jimmy did was play basketball and go to school. He had to go to school to play on the high school team - so he went, but he didn't really like it.

Jimmy finished this night with jumping drills. He would jump and hang onto the rim in a variety of ways. One leg, one hand. One leg, two hands. Two legs, one hand and so forth and so on. Also, every night he would try to dunk the ball, although he had never actually succeeded. "One day," he thought to himself, "I'm going to slam just like Sleepy Phillips." After these final drills, Jimmy started his twenty minute walk through the dark and lonely streets of St. Louis, back to his small house on South 22nd Street.

Jimmy never really liked just hanging out like some of the guys he would see while walking home. "Too boring," he thought. "Thank God for basketball," Jimmy had said to himself more than a few times.

As Harold Phillips was hanging up his telephone, he thought about how crazy his life had become. Harold had just finished speaking with Gus Williams, his hometown buddy. Gus had called to set up a golf game for Saturday morning and had made a point of reminding Harold that it had been ten months since they had last played together. Harold was remembering the days when he and Gus used to play every weekend. "Shoot," he thought to himself, "I need to make more time for the things I really enjoy." He quickly put this thought out of his mind though, just as he had thousands of times before.

Harold Phillips' life had become extremely busy the last few years. Some people wanted him for one thing, others for something else. It had gotten to the point where he had no time for his family or himself, but these last few years were only the crest of a wave that had been building for quite some time. Ever since he had walked onto the University of St. Louis' basketball floor to play his first college game, Harold Phillips had ceased living a normal life. Those who saw that first game knew right away that the tall and slender, yet powerful young man possessed athletic ability of the greatest degree, although no one could have predicted the stature he had attained by the end of his playing days.

Sports writers dubbed him "the greatest player of all time." Corporations lined up to have him sponsor their products. Harold Phillips became an international superstar, achieving all the riches and fame that went with this status.

Harold never used to dream about fame and fortune while growing up, but he did spend many hours dreaming about playing basketball. As a boy he had idolized Julius Erving, just like everybody else. He spent one whole summer working in the meat packing plant just to earn enough money to buy Converse sneakers, just like Dr. J.'s. Harold would try to emulate Dr. J.'s fluid leaping ability which always resulted in pretty drives down the lane and ended with the patented "tomahawk jam," although, until he was older, Harold just laid the ball in.

"Sleepy," that's what all the guys back in the neighborhood called Harold, was different from all the other kids that idolized Julius Erving. Sleepy had set his mind on becoming just as good as him, but a funny thing happened. He became better. Sleepy's career read like a childhood storybook. St. Louis High School City Championship, Missouri High School State Championship, two NCAA championships, seven NBA championships and three Olympic gold medals. Sleepy had retired two years ago, leaving behind only memories for school-yard kids to dream about.

The dreams were easy, but reality was much tougher to control. Sleepy's life was one most people envied, but they didn't know the whole story. The cameras, autograph seekers, commercials and all the other trappings of fame had put a drain on his time and energy. His life had become a constant publicity tour. Everywhere he went he was mobbed by fans. Even though all the people were kind and generous with their admiration, Sleepy yearned for privacy. He wished for the kind of normal life he had lived as a young boy in St. Louis. It had gotten so bad lately that he couldn't walk outside without bodyguards.

It was tough on Sleepy, but it was even tougher on his family. He knew that his wife and two daughters would be better off without all the attention. It seemed he had lost control of his life, but Harold "Sleepy" Phillips had made up his mind - starting Saturday morning on the golf course he was going to regain control.

CHAPTER II

The Meeting

Golf was the only sport that never came easily to Sleepy. It frustrated him greatly that he could not dictate where the small ball would go. He was a natural at all other sports, but at golf, no way. His best score ever was 79, but he usually scored in the high 80's. Sleepy figured this was not nearly good enough for the man many considered the greatest athlete in America.

Today, however, he was playing just for fun. Sleepy had been looking forward to this Saturday morning ever since his old buddy, Gus, had called at the beginning of the week. Sleepy could not believe that it had been ten months since he and Gus had last played.

Every Saturday morning Jimmy made it a point to be the first caddy to the golf course. This way he got the first group of golfers in the morning, enabling him to be on the basketball court by noon. Tony Mendez, his boss, assigned caddies to the golfers. He liked Jimmy's attitude, so he always obliged Jimmy and assigned him to the first group.

"Jimmy," Tony said with a big smile when he saw his young employee, "big surprise for you today, buddy."

"What's the surprise?" Jimmy asked as he parked his bike in the caddie's garage.

"You'll see. Now go ahead with the first group. They're waiting at the first tee."

Tony was still smiling from ear to ear as Jimmy walked towards the first tee. As Jimmy approached the golfers, he stopped dead in his tracks. Jimmy stared at the two men in front of him.

"You're Sleepy Phillips," he said to Sleepy.

"Yes I am, kid. Who are you?"

Jimmy didn't answer, he just stared. Sleepy Phillips was Jimmy's idol. He used to watch him play on television all the time. Even though Sleepy had retired two years ago, Jimmy still considered him the greatest.

"Jimmy, Jimmy," Tony yelled. "Wake up and carry the man's bag. He's waiting." Both Sleepy and Gus Williams began to laugh out loud.

"Are you okay?" Sleepy asked as he patted Jimmy on the shoulder.

"Yes sir. I'm sorry. I'm just a little surprised."

"No problem," Sleepy replied gently.

"Tony, if you don't mind, I'll carry both bags," Jimmy said questioningly as he quickly regained his senses, along with the strength in his legs.

"I sort of figured you would say that. Go ahead, they're all yours," Tony answered.

"This here is my good friend, Gus Williams," Sleepy said to Jimmy as he patted Gus on the back.

"How are you doing, sir? My name is Jimmy Feen."

"Nice to meet you, Jimmy," Gus greeted him.

"Okay, let's play some golf," Sleepy said.

Sleepy was about to tee off on the first hole when he told Jimmy to get him the 2-iron instead of the driver. Sleepy couldn't hit his driver on the first hole and he knew it. Jimmy retrieved the new club and ran it over to Sleepy.

"Here's your two iron, sir."

Sleepy took a long fluid swing, accelerating through the ball and drove it on a straight path down the middle of the fairway. It went like this for Sleepy all day. Everything he hit was perfect. Jimmy ran after every divot, had every ball cleaned and every club ready. He was doing a great job and Sleepy was noticing.

"Hey, kid, you're doing a fine job. You might be the reason I'm shooting so well. Keep working this hard and you're going to make a lot of money someday."

"Hopefully, I can play basketball just like you," Jimmy replied. By the time Sleepy and Gus reached the tee box for the 17th hole, they were tired. Even though Sleepy was a well-conditioned athlete, it had been a while since he had last played golf. The 17th hole was a 159-yard par three. Sleepy had a 7-iron in his hands and was getting ready to swing.

Jimmy had noticed Sleepy getting more and more tired throughout the morning, and without thinking, he blurted out, "Mr. Phillips, I think you might want to use a six iron."

Gus laughed and joked with Sleepy. "The kid is telling you how to play now. I'll bet he has a better swing than you do." Gus was kidding, but he also wanted to beat Sleepy at golf this morning and the two good friends were not above needling each other.

Sleepy laughed out loud. "Yeah, yeah, next the kid will be telling me how to shoot foul shots." Jimmy chuckled inside. He remembered that Sleepy's only weakness on the basketball court was foul shooting.

Sleepy addressed the ball, the 7-iron still in his hands. After a few shakes and wiggles, he put a smooth, effortless swing into the ball. However, just as Jimmy had noticed, Sleepy didn't follow through completely, a sure giveaway of fatigue. The ball fell into a sand trap about ten yards short of the green. After Gus had hit onto the green, Sleepy walked to his ball. Jimmy followed closely behind.

"You think you're pretty smart, don't you?" Sleepy said jokingly to Jimmy as they walked to the ball.

"No, sir," Jimmy replied seriously. "I just noticed that you were getting a little tired at the end of your swing."

"Do you have any advice on how to get out of this sand trap?" Sleepy asked skeptically.

"Well, I have seen a few people putt it out. It's one of the toughest traps on the course." Sleepy scoffed a bit. He had never seen anyone use a putter out of any sand trap before. Sleepy told Jimmy to hand him the sand wedge. After a few practice swings Sleepy hit the ball, but it fell well short of the hole. He muttered something under his breath.

Sleepy then told Jimmy to hand him the putter and another ball. Sleepy dropped the ball into the trap and hit it with the putter. Gus watched in amusement as the ball rolled over the top of the sand trap, onto the green and finally came to rest six inches from the hole. This was how Jimmy had seen it done before.

Gus burst into laughter. "This kid should be playing and you should be carrying his clubs," he chided his buddy.

After finishing the 17th hole, the two old friends were tied. They decided to bet on the last hole. Loser would buy the sodas in the clubhouse. As Gus was teeing his ball up, Jimmy had an idea. He knew he needed to act fast.

"Excuse me, do you mind if I get into this bet?" Jimmy asked, breaking Gus' concentration.

Both men were surprised by this. Sleepy was a little angry and after a few moments he replied, "Jimmy, you can bet, but if you lose you have to give all the money you make today to another caddy." Sleepy figured he might as well teach this kid a lesson.

Jimmy figured his tip would be around seventy-five dollars, taking into account that Sleepy was a rich man and would probably tip well.

"I'll take the bet," Jimmy answered, deciding the risk was well worth the possible pay off, "but if I beat you, you have to come say hello to my basketball team before our game Monday night." Gus was laughing so hard he nearly knocked over his golf bag.

"You're something else, kid," Sleepy laughed. "Let's do it." Gus teed off first and drove his ball about 275 yards down the right-hand side of the fairway.

"You're next," Sleepy said to Jimmy.

Jimmy had been loosening up off to the side. He motioned to Sleepy that he was going to use Sleepy's driver. Sleepy nodded his approval. After taking the club, Jimmy realized it was a little too long for him, so he made the proper adjustments.

"Keep your head down," he told himself. Jimmy took two practice swings and then swung at the ball, hitting it solidly. The ball took off on a low, straight trajectory. It finally settled 250 yards down the center of the fairway. Both men were impressed.

"Good shot," they said in unison.

Sleepy teed off last and hit the ball about five yards further than Jimmy. As they approached their golf balls, Sleepy used a technique he had used on opponents many times before. He tried to unnerve Jimmy.

"Now don't get nervous," Sleepy prodded him. "This is where the real players prove themselves."

Jimmy just smiled. He knew his own abilities and that this shot was just a smooth 5-iron. Again, Jimmy patiently took his two practice swings and then hit the ball. It traveled beautifully towards the hole, rising high above the fairway and then dropping lazily to the green. It spun slightly backwards and stopped ten feet away from the hole.

Sleepy swung next. He also hit a good shot, but the ball came to rest about fifteen feet away from the hole. Gus also hit to the green leaving himself a thirty-foot putt. Because he was furthest away, Gus putted first. He made a nice putt leaving only a tap-in for his par four.

Sleepy putted next and when he missed the first putt and made the second, he also tallied a four. Sleepy continued his psych job as he walked off the green.

"Well, kid, if you don't make this, we tie and nobody wins," he said. Jimmy didn't even hear Sleepy's attempt to bait him. He knew that if he made this putt, everybody on his basketball team would faint when they saw Sleepy Phillips walk into the locker room. As Jimmy approached his ball to putt, he whispered so that Gus and Sleepy couldn't hear him. "God, I promise I'll stop swearing if I can just make this one putt," Jimmy prayed.

By this time, Gus was rooting for Jimmy. He just laughed as Sleepy tried to psych Jimmy out. Jimmy took his two practice swings and then confidently swung his putter at the ball. The ball rolled straight at the hole and then at the last minute broke suddenly to the left. The ball hit the edge of the hole, spun completely around and then finally dropped in for a birdie three. Jimmy had won the bet. He pumped his fist with excitement.

"Good shot, kid," Sleepy said with a sarcastic tone, suddenly realizing that he was going to have to live up to his side of the bet.

Jimmy and Sleepy talked in the clubhouse afterward. Jimmy gave Sleepy the name of his high school and the time the game started.

"You have to be there an hour early or our coach won't let you in," Jimmy warned him.

Sleepy smiled and assured Jimmy he would be there. He then took a hundred dollar bill out of his wallet and handed it to Jimmy. "Start a bank account kid, you're going to need it."

"I already have one," Jimmy said with a confident smile.

"I'm not surprised," Sleepy muttered. Sleepy then made his way to his car. He signed a few autographs along the way and then quickly ducked into the driver's seat of his Mercedes. Gus was sitting in the passenger's seat, still laughing as the two old friends drove away.

CHAPTER III

A Call To Coaching

Memories of his old high school days came rushing back to Sleepy as he drove into the parking lot of George Washington Carver High School. Carver High was located in downtown St. Louis.

Sleepy noticed the atmosphere of high school basketball had not changed much since he had played. There were a few kids running around outside of the gym. Cheerleaders were practicing their jumps in the courtyard out front and an elderly woman was setting up a table at which to collect the two dollar admission. She never even noticed as Sleepy laid his money on the table and walked past her into the gym.

Sleepy figured Jimmy played on the freshman team since there were hardly any people around. A few school kids walked into the gym behind Sleepy. When they saw who was standing in front of them, they pointed and whispered.

"Yes, you're right. I am Sleepy Phillips," Sleepy wanted to scream at them, but he didn't. "Hopefully, I can get out of here before too many people show up," Sleepy thought to himself.

Sleepy saw the door marked "Home Team" in the corner of the gym. As he walked inside, Sleepy prepared himself for autographs and awestruck kids, but instead he walked into silence. This was odd. Most locker rooms he had been in were filled with good natured jokes and music. There was none of this here, just silence. As Sleepy ventured inside the locker room, he saw nine young men huddled around a chalkboard with a look of confusion settling over the whole group. Sleepy saw Jimmy standing off to the side.

"Hey, Jimmy," Sleepy said in a loud voice. Jimmy quickly turned around and, as he saw his hero standing in the doorway, he broke into a big smile. He walked over to Sleepy. At the same time all the other kids turned and looked. Their eyes opened wide and they stared.

"I knew you'd show up," a relieved Jimmy said. None of his teammates had believed his golfing story. "This here is Sleepy Phillips!" he proclaimed proudly to everyone. At once, all the kids came and tried to shake his hand. Sleepy obliged and shook them all. After a few minutes of this unabashed admiration, the youngsters settled down.

"Well, what time does the game start?" Sleepy asked. As if on cue, all the boys became sullen and quiet again. Many of them walked back to their seats and sat down. Sleepy was confused. "What's going on?" he asked Jimmy.

"Our coach is in the hospital. They think he had a heart attack. Now we don't have a coach," Jimmy answered.

"What about the assistant coaches?" Sleepy asked.

"Don't have any," a small kid in the back replied.

"We were just trying to decide who would start," Jimmy stated. "This is our first game, but we figured we could coach ourselves until the varsity coach gets here."

Sleepy felt horrible for these young men. Their first game as high school freshman and they had no coach. He looked around the room and saw these young, bewildered faces. Before he had entirely thought the situation through, Sleepy let his emotions get the best of him.

"I have a better idea," Sleepy said. "I'll coach you until the varsity coach arrives."

The boys voiced their approval unanimously. Instinctively, Sleepy took charge.

"First of all, everyone out on the floor. Split into two lines under your own basket and do some lay-ups. No outside shots, only lay-ups!" Sleepy instructed them. The young men let out a cheer of enthusiasm and ran onto the floor. Jimmy was the last one out.

"Thanks a lot Mr. Phillips. I know this wasn't part of the bet," Jimmy said as he ran out the door.

"Don't worry about it, kid. Focus on the game," Sleepy said assuredly as he patted Jimmy on the back. Jimmy ran out with the rest of the team, leaving Sleepy alone in an old, dirty, high school locker room. "What have I gotten myself into?" he laughed to himself. Sleepy breathed a long sigh, took a drink from the rusty water fountain and then headed out to yet another basketball floor.

There was no burst of energy as he opened the door. The bleachers had, at most, fifty people in them. There was no band and the cheerleaders weren't even paying attention. Sleepy walked onto the floor and began to watch his new team do their drills. The visitor's locker room door opened and the opposing team came out while Sleepy was in the middle of the court. When they saw him standing there, they all stopped and stared. The opposing coach made his way out the door, pushing and shoving his players ahead.

"Move it. Move it. What's the hold up?" he yelled at them, but when he saw Sleepy he also stopped and stared. After about fifteen seconds, the coach came to Sleepy and asked, "Aren't you Sleepy Phillips?"

"Yes I am," Sleepy replied. "The regular coach is in the hospital and I'm coaching until the varsity coach arrives. I'll explain the whole story later." Sleepy shook the opposing coach's hand and walked away.

The opposing team went into their lay-up drill, although most of the players still had their eyes on Sleepy. Sleepy walked under the Eagles' basket and continued watching his team. He felt as if everyone in the gym was looking at him, and he was right.

The Eagles broke into four separate lines at the corners of the half court and started doing a passing drill. They drilled the ball back and forth to each other and then switched lines. After about four minutes, they broke into three even lines and performed the weave drill with the last guy laying the ball in the basket.

Sleepy's eyes fixed on Jimmy. It was the fluidness of Jimmy's motion that caught Sleepy's attention. Jimmy dribbled twice, spun into the lane and then switched the ball from his right to his left hand while doing a reverse lay-up on the other side of the rim. The shot was pretty, but even more impressive was the ease with which it was performed.

Sleepy sized up his team and realized they had a good mix of height and speed. But as Sleepy knew, with no teamwork, there is no team. The horn sounded and players from both teams headed for their respective benches.

Sleepy could hear the whispers. Everyone in the gym was wondering if it was really Harold "Sleepy" Phillips coaching Carver High's ninth grade squad and if it was, why was he doing it? The kids sat on the bench, their heads turned to Sleepy, looking to him for leadership.

"Who is the captain of this team?" Sleepy asked.

"I am," Jimmy answered. Sleepy was not surprised.

"Who are the starters?" he asked Jimmy.

"Well, this is the first game, but I think coach was planning on starting me, Kenny, Too Tall, Bull and Jonesy."

Sleepy realized he only knew the name of one of his players and that was Jimmy. "Okay, you boys get on the floor. Everybody else sit down," Sleepy ordered. Sleepy huddled the starting five around him, close to the center of the floor. "Fellas, play tough defense. Defense wins games." Sleepy laughed to himself. Those were the same words his old college coach used to say.

As Sleepy walked back to the bench, he could see that the stands were now filling up and everyone was looking straight at him. Some pointed while others boldly called out to him. Sleepy smiled, waved and then quickly sat down.

As the players on both teams were getting ready for the opening tip, Sleepy sized up his starting five. Kenny looked to be no taller than 5' 4", but his hair made him look five inches taller. "Everybody needs an identity," Sleepy reasoned.

Too Tall was perfectly described by his nickname. He looked to be about 6' 7". His glasses were about 3/4" thick and his feet looked to be three sizes too big for his body.

Sleepy figured Bull should have been a wrestler. He was built like a brick wall. About 5' 9" tall and 180 pounds, Bull looked older than fifteen. Jonesy was thin, but wiry. A good mix for a small forward.

Finally, Sleepy focused on Jimmy. Jimmy stood about six feet tall with long arms and long legs. However, what struck Sleepy most about Jimmy was something he had noticed at the golf course, his inner confidence. It seemed that most of the other boys were focusing on the opposing players, while Jimmy was rubbing his hands together, deep in thought about what he had to do.

"Hello, Mr. Phillips," the referee said, breaking Sleepy's train of thought. "The other coach told us you would explain at halftime why you're here. That's good enough for us. Let's play ball."

As Too Tall lined up for the jump ball, Sleepy looked around at the small gym and thought about the situation he had gotten himself into. "Might as well make the most of it," he reasoned.

The opposing center out jumped Too Tall for the ball and tapped it to his forward. The forward turned and rifled a pass to a guard, who was cutting in from the wing. The guard converted the pass into an easy lay-up. A perfect tip play. Bull retrieved the ball and passed it into Kenny. Sleepy nearly broke out laughing as he watched Kenny dribble the ball. He pounded the ball on the floor as if he was trying to knock the air out of it. The defensive man was not guarding him close, but Kenny still switched the ball from hand to hand. It looked like he was trying to impersonate Curley Neal, the old Harlem Globetrotter dribbling wizard.

The opposing team was in a "2-3 zone defense." Kenny yelled out the "number two" play. He passed the ball to Jimmy who was cutting away from the basket on the left side of the floor. Jimmy dribbled to the corner, faked a pass back to Kenny and then bounced a pass into Too Tall, who had set up on the low block. Too Tall dribbled the ball into the lane, where it was quickly stolen by the opposing team's center. The opposing team quickly pushed the ball to the other end of the court.

The attacking guards were quick to spot some indecision on the part of the Eagles' defense and ran a series of baseline picks for their main scorer. While Bull and Jonesy argued who should guard him, the opposing player executed a backdoor cut and scored an easy lay-up.

The entire first quarter proceeded the same way. The opposing team capitalized on Eagles' turnovers and then ran well-designed picks and screens on the offensive end. Sleepy's squad looked confused. The offense looked like a school yard pick-up game with each player receiving a pass and then looking to score all by himself. No one was passing to the open man and there was no picking of the defensive players.

Defensively, their level of effort was excellent, but again, organization was lacking. If two boys were playing man-to-man defense the other three were playing zone. The Eagles were showing little basketball savvy and this was making for a lopsided game.

One thing that did stand out to Sleepy was the determination these youngsters had. Even though they were being beaten badly, they continued to play tough, clawing defense and hustled after every loose ball. The fundamentals were lacking, but the Eagles had talent and good work habits. "These kids just need a little direction," Sleepy thought. At the end of the first quarter, the Eagles trailed 27-11.

Jimmy had scored six points, all on lay-ups. Jonesy scored the other five with outside shots, one being a three-pointer. As the team came to the bench before the second quarter, they looked depressed. Sleepy substituted the four remaining bench players for Too Tall, Jonesy, Kenny and Bull. This left Jimmy to play with the four substitutes.

As the second quarter wore on, the opposing team continued its heady offensive play and used solid defense to continue its domination of the Eagles. The Eagles scored only six more points to fall behind by the score of 47-17.

As the boys headed to the locker room for halftime, Sleepy noticed that the bleachers were beginning to fill up with spectators in anticipation of the varsity game. Shouts of "Sleepy, what are you doing here?" filled the gym. The fans could not believe that the superstar they saw on television was coaching their ninth grade team. As Sleepy walked into the locker room, a man came up and introduced himself as Principal Ferguson.

"Mr. Phillips, I'm very thankful that you helped the kids and the school by coaching our team. I got a call from the hospital and the regular coach is doing fine, although he won't be able to return this season." The entire team let out a sigh of relief upon hearing that their regular coach would be okay. "The varsity coach just arrived and I explained the situation to him." The principal, who was a large man with a large belly, started to laugh. "I should say, I tried to explain the situation, but I really don't even know why you're here."

Before Sleepy could explain, Kenny stood up and told Principal Ferguson the whole story.

"Am I to understand that you're here because you lost a golf bet to one of our players?" Principal Ferguson asked Sleepy with a laugh.

"Yep," Sleepy replied with a straight face.

"Okay," Ferguson said with an amused smile. "Now, as I was saying, we are grateful to you for filling in. The varsity coach is going to coach the second half. Sorry you had to stay longer than you planned, but thanks again."

"I can't leave now. We have to come back and win this game. I'd like to stay, if that's all right with you," Sleepy said with a determined look.

Principal Ferguson shook Sleepy's hand and said, "No problem."

Sleepy looked around at each one of the players. "First of all, thank God that your coach is going to be fine. However, if he knew how you boys were playing, he might not feel so good after all," he joked. With that, the team began to loosen up.

Sleepy continued, "I've decided to stay for the rest of the game and be your coach, but we've got to get something straight right now. You have to play as a team, not as a bunch of individuals. This team right here in this locker room has talent. You're more talented than the team you're playing, but you're not playing together. Your hustle is good. All of you play hard, and that's admirable, but I learned a long time ago that individuals lose, teams win."

"Here's what we're going to do," Sleepy said as he walked toward the chalkboard. "We're going to play half-court, man-to-man press defense. This takes a huge amount of determination and communication. If your man beats you to the hoop, somebody has to help by rotating over."

"On offense we're going to try two different sets. Against a zone defense, I want you to set up in a triangle offense." Sleepy pointed at Bull and said, "You will play the post position." Then he pointed at Jonesy, "You'll play the top corner and Jimmy will run the baseline."

"The important thing to remember is to move without the ball. Also, when you drive to the hoop, look for another person to pass to for an easier shot," Sleepy said, continuing his halftime speech.

"Against the man-to-man defense, I want you," he pointed at Kenny as he said this, "to handle the ball and to look continuously for screens and picks. The guy picking your man should then roll to the basket. Put your hands up and be ready for the ball," Sleepy told everyone.

Sleepy was taking charge and it seemed to be working. The players were listening intently and Sleepy could see they were starting to get pumped up. He slowly repeated everything he had just said, but this time he used the chalkboard as a visual reinforcement. After he finished, Sleepy instructed everybody to huddle in a close circle. Sleepy knew that the only way they could win this game was to have their emotions boiling. He began his pep talk.

"Well, what do you want to do? You have two choices. You can play the same as before and hope you win or you can go out there and set your minds on winning. What do you want to do?" The entire team screamed that they wanted to win.

"The only way you're going to win this game is to play tough defense, look for teammates who have better shots and communicate with each other." His voice started to grow louder. "I think you can do it, but you have to commit. Commit to yourselves and to each other that you're part of a team and that your team wants to win. Are you ready to commit yourselves?" Again, the boys screamed their answer, only this time it was louder. At that moment, a referee came into the locker room to order the Eagles back out to the floor.

"You heard the man. Get out there!" Sleepy roared. The players ran out of the locker room like a team ahead by twenty points rather than one down by thirty. They were jumping up and down and slamming the walls as they left the locker room.

When Sleepy stepped out of the locker room and back into the gymnasium, the crowd erupted in cheers. The stands were now filled and everybody was staring at him. Sleepy hurried to the bench, waved, and then sat down.

The fans behind Sleepy couldn't believe the best basketball player of all time was sitting right in front of them. They began tapping him on the shoulder to ask for autographs. Many simply asked for an explanation why he was there. Finally, Principal Ferguson came with two security guards and had them sit down in the stands directly behind Sleepy.

"I don't think anybody is going to bother you now," Ferguson said to Sleepy.

"Thanks," Sleepy replied. The horn sounded and the two teams headed back to their benches for last-minute instructions.

"Okay guys," Sleepy started, "same starting five. Remember, hustle, hustle, hustle! Find the open man and communicate. If you commit to playing as a team, you can come back and win this game. You have the talent."

The Eagles retained possession from the first half. Bull passed into Kenny who dribbled the ball up the court. Recognizing a zone defense as he reached half court, Kenny called for the triangle offensive which Sleepy had showed them at halftime. Sleepy laughed out loud as he saw his team trying to run an offense that professional teams had difficulty executing.

Kenny passed the ball into Too Tall, who had lined up in the low post. Too Tall passed back to Jimmy, who was positioned in the corner. Jimmy quickly swung the ball around by passing to Bull, who was standing at the top of the key. Jimmy curled around Too Tall, putting his hand up as he broke free from his defensive opponent. Bull saw the opening and rifled a pass to Jimmy underneath the basket. Jimmy jumped, caught the ball in midair, and gracefully laid it into the basket with his left hand. A perfectly executed play which had Sleepy standing and cheering.

Just as Sleepy had instructed at halftime, the Eagles started their defense at half court, trapping and hustling all over the floor. The other team was caught off guard by the tough play and began to get a little wild with their passes. Jimmy, sensing that his man was about to receive a pass, jumped in front of him and stole the ball. He raced the other way for an easy two points.

Sleepy pointed at Junior Hernandez to enter the game in place of Too Tall. As soon as Junior checked in, he stole the ball and hit Bull with a perfect pass under the basket, which Bull easily converted into two points. The Eagles had listened to their substitute coach and were playing inspired, team basketball. They kept up this style of play the entire third quarter and when the period had ended, they found themselves down by only fourteen points, 55-41.

To the fans in the stands, it was an unbelievable sight. World-famous athlete Sleepy Phillips was sweating through a thousand dollar suit, exhorting their freshman team to "Play hard and play as a team!"

At the end of the third quarter, the boys came to the bench. "Great quarter," Sleepy congratulated them. "The other team is getting tired and I can definitely feel the momentum switching. I know you can come back and win this game." To keep the adrenaline pumping, Sleepy had the boys huddle in close to him and he said with a hushed voice, "Boys, if you really want to win this game, you have to put everything else out of your minds. Think basketball only. Lose yourself in the game. Dive for loose balls, hustle on defense," and then he repeated himself, "lose yourself in the game. Lose yourself in the game." As play began for the fourth quarter, the Eagles were a group of young men thinking about only one thing, winning this basketball game. Sleepy had inspired them.

The other coach had also made a few adjustments. Sensing the momentum switch, he instructed his team to stall in order to run time off the clock. Sleepy recognized the play and quickly countered this offensive maneuver by having Kenny and Jonesy deny their men the ball, thus forcing the man with the ball to pass to a forward or center. This full-court pressure resulted in a few steals, but Sleepy knew that time was running out on his team, so he signaled for a timeout.

"We have to start fouling," Sleepy began. "Try to foul the center, but foul whoever you can, because time is precious. Hopefully, they'll miss their foul shots." This plan worked well as the Eagles either stole the ball or collected the rebounds of missed foul shots for the next three minutes. On offense, Jimmy just flat out took over the game. Because the other team was playing zone defense, Jimmy hung to the outside and hit two 3-pointers. They quickly switched to man-to-man defense in order to guard Jimmy more closely, but Jimmy easily drove by the defenders for easy lay-ups or passes to open teammates. Jimmy was displaying a natural athletic ability for the game that had Sleepy shaking his head in amazement.

The fans watching the game were going crazy. For some reason unknown to them, Sleepy Phillips was coaching their ninth grade team to an amazing comeback. Sleepy wasn't being subdued either. He was walking up and down the sideline, hands waving, encouraging his team to play harder. He too had lost himself in the game.

The Eagles were playing fanatic defense and as the last minute of the game began to tick off the clock, Junior stole the ball from his man and passed to Jimmy, who was breaking for the other basket. In perfect stride, Jimmy caught the ball and then took two long steps before jumping towards the basket. He took off on a long, slow climb to the basket and to the amazement of everybody watching the game, he kept rising until his head was almost even with the rim. Jimmy laid the ball softly into the basket. The Eagles were now down by only one point. The opposing team continued to stall time off the clock. Thirty seconds, twenty-five, twenty, the clock ticked down.

"Foul, foul," Sleepy yelled from the sideline.

Jimmy realized the clock was running down, so he let his man dribble past him. With the quickness that all schoolyard players have witnessed before, Jimmy then whipped his arm around the back of his man, knocking the ball forward. Kenny happened to be standing in just the right spot and caught the loose ball. Jimmy broke to the half-court line and put his hands up. Kenny saw him the whole way and zipped him a perfect pass.

Just as Jimmy was turning towards the basket, he stole a quick glance at the clock. Five seconds, four seconds it ticked down. Jimmy started dribbling for the basket, but something inside told him he didn't have enough time for a lay-up. Instead, he pulled up for a jump shot just inside the three-point line and as he let the ball go, the buzzer sounded. The ball spun lazily towards the hoop with a high arc. As Jimmy told his friends later, he heard the whole gym go silent. Finally, the ball dropped into the net.

The stands exploded in excitement. The Eagles ran around the court looking for one another to hug, as if they had just won the NCAA Championship game. Fans were exchanging high fives, talking about the best comeback they had ever seen. Sleepy Phillips was left standing silent, by himself. For the first time all night, the eyes were not on him. He looked around the small gym and smiled as he saw the excitement around him.

Sleepy made his way past the cheering fans to the locker room. He waved to the crowd of people, then ducked inside the locker room door. Once inside, he saw nine very happy young men.

"Great game, fellas!" Sleepy said loudly, his emotions still high. "You have a lot of talent here, but you have even more desire and toughness. I'm very impressed by the way you guys came back. You have a lot to be proud of. I had a great time tonight and I want to thank you all. Now hit the showers. You deserve it."

"Excuse me, Sleepy," Jimmy interrupted. "I would, on behalf of all the guys, like to thank you for coaching us. I know you didn't have to stay, but we appreciate it." The entire team thanked Sleepy. Sleepy was overwhelmed with emotions for these young men.

"It was my pleasure," he said before turning to leave. When he opened the gym door there was a crowd of people waiting for him. Sleepy told them politely that he was tired and just wanted to go home. The security guards cleared a path for him through the adoring fans. As he walked through the parking lot and got into his car, he turned to look back. People were still watching him. "What a crazy night," Sleepy thought as he started his car and headed home.

CHAPTER IV

Fantasy Coach

Bull McKinnon, Tommy Peterson, Kenny James, Junior Hernandez, Edgar "Jonesy" Jones and Jimmy Feen always walked the same way home from school. Even though it wasn't the shortest route, they took it because they could look at all the big houses by the lake. On most nights they would look at the houses and dream about having enough money to afford one, but this night was different. The six friends hardly even noticed the big houses and the expensive cars. They were still flabbergasted that the great Sleepy Phillips had actually coached their team.

"Sleepy Phillips, can you believe it?" Kenny said.

"I would have loved to just meet him, but this was unbelievable," Tommy added.

"Yeah," Jimmy said, "but I feel a little bad because I think he got more than he bargained for. I know he didn't plan on spending the whole night here."

"I'm sorry something happened to Coach Jackson," Junior joined in, "but I'm glad Sleepy Phillips was the substitute coach."

"Me too," Jonesy agreed.

Bull was kicking a stone as he walked and all the guys knew that when he did this, he was deep in thought.

"What's going through your muscle cramped brain?" Kenny finally asked him.

Bull shrugged off the good-natured insult. "I was just wondering who was going to coach the team now that Coach Jackson is going to be in the hospital for a while."

"I don't know, but I sure wish it would be Sleepy Phillips," Jimmy replied. All the boys agreed with that.

"You have been thinking about those kids all night, haven't you?" Sandra Phillips asked her husband. "I wish I had been there. It must have been a sight to see."

"Believe me, it was," Sleepy sighed. "Those kids are really special. They hustled and fought. I was really proud of them. They could have given up, but they didn't." Sleepy paused for a few moments and then added, "They were just real good kids. Jimmy, that kid I bet on the golf course, he has real talent. With some hard work, I believe he could make it to the NBA. Coaching those kids tonight made me feel so alive. I didn't have to worry about being anywhere or how I was acting or who I needed to talk to. All I had to worry about was teaching those kids the game of basketball."

"You've been saying you wanted to coach ever since you retired. Here's your chance," Sandra suggested.

Sleepy didn't say anything, he just stared at the wall. Sandra had seen that look before, but not since her husband had retired from the NBA. She knew he missed the competition and, more importantly, the game itself. She kissed him on the cheek and then went upstairs to check on their two daughters. She knew her husband would do the right thing.

On Tuesday morning the entire school was filled with talk of how Sleepy Phillips had coached the team the night before. Everyone in the administrative offices had gathered in the main lobby. Even Principal Ferguson, who was usually all business during school hours, was sitting on a desk, talking about the game.

"I couldn't believe it," Stan Marcello, Dean of Students, said. "I walked into the gym and there was Sleepy Phillips standing by the bench, yelling at our kids to get their hands up. How in the world did we get Sleepy Phillips to replace Coach Jackson?"

"A young man named Jimmy Feen is responsible for that," stated an unfamiliar voice. All those in the room turned around and stared in amazement at Sleepy Phillips, who was standing just inside the door.

"Sleepy Phillips," Principal Ferguson said in an excited voice, "what are you doing here?"

"I'd like to talk to you about that in private, if I could," Sleepy replied.

"Okay, step right this way," a stunned Principal Ferguson answered as he made his way to his office.

The staff members in the administrative offices knew the principal to be a carefree person, always with a kind word for people. However, they had never seen him smile quite so radiantly. He was beaming from ear to ear as he walked out of his office about ten minutes later with Sleepy following behind him.

"It's going to be a pleasure working with you. If there's anything I can do, please, don't hesitate to call," Ferguson said to Sleepy.

"Thank you very much," Sleepy replied.

The two men shook hands. Sleepy waved goodbye to everyone in the offices before ducking his head as he passed underneath the doorway. At once, everyone in the office started asking questions. Principal Ferguson was barely able to keep the smile off his face as he explained the situation to everyone.

Jimmy was sitting in U.S. History class, bored as usual. His teacher was lecturing on the Pilgrims' settlement in America. This was the third straight day on the subject and by now, Jimmy had had enough. He was not bored with the material really, but bored by the way the teacher taught it. She read directly from the textbook in a monotone voice. Boring!

As usual, Jimmy began daydreaming about playing basketball in the NBA. Today, however, his thoughts kept coming back to reality and to Sleepy Phillips. He still couldn't believe that his favorite basketball player in the whole world had coached his team last night. It was too unreal. He thought about his regular coach and felt relieved that Coach Jackson was going to be all right, but he started wondering who was going to coach the team for the rest of the season. "Most likely Coach Vasic, the assistant varsity coach," Jimmy thought before the lunch bell interrupted his thoughts. He grabbed his books and dashed out the door to meet up with Bull, Kenny, Tommy and the rest of the guys for lunch.

"Bull, you're going to grow into two people if you keep eating like that," Kenny teased Bull as the group of friends sat down at the lunch table. Bull's plate had double everything. Double lasagna, double beans, double rice, double milk. Bull was legendary for his eating ability.

"You're just jealous cause the more you eat the smaller you get," Bull snapped back.

This seemed to hurt Kenny. He was self-conscious about his height, but he recovered quickly and joked to Jimmy, "What about you, superstar? What are you thinking about?"

"I was just thinking about the game last night and the way we all played as a team in the second half. It was great. I sure wish Sleepy could coach the rest of our games."

All the boys at the table thought about that for a moment. As they ate their lunches and listened to the talk around the cafeteria, they were surprised to hear everyone talking about their team and Sleepy Phillips. It seemed as if the whole school saw the game. A couple of older guys even came over to their table and congratulated them on the comeback, which was unusual because most ninth graders sat in obscurity during lunch.

"I'll bet Coach Vasic will take over as coach," Too Tall said, resuming the conversation.

"Probably right about that, Too Tall," Bull muttered.

"I agree with Jimmy. I wish Sleepy Phillips would coach the whole season," Kenny said.

"You should have bet the man for the whole season," Junior said to Jimmy. All the guys laughed, including Jimmy.

When the bell sounded, the friends all dumped their trays and headed back to class. Jimmy broke off from the group to head to science class. As he was walking into class, one of his classmates asked him why Sleepy Phillips was at the school today.

"You've got it all wrong," Jimmy told him. "Sleepy was at our game last night."

"I know he was at the game last night, but I also saw him walking out of the administrative offices this morning," Jimmy's classmate retorted.

"No fooling?" Jimmy inquired, suddenly mystified.

"Straight up. Guess you don't know. Anyway, great game last night."

"Thanks," Jimmy said.

As class was about to begin, the intercom squawked and the announcer said, "Would the ninth grade basketball team please report to the locker room directly after classes today. Thank you." Jimmy daydreamed the rest of the day.

Bull and Jimmy walked together to the locker room after school. The varsity players had just finished dressing and were headed to the floor for practice.

"Anybody know what's going on?" Jonesy asked as he walked into the locker room.

"I think we're going to find out now," Junior replied as he pointed to Principal Ferguson, who had just walked in through the door.

Ferguson was deceptively large. Because of his weight, he did not look tall until you stood next to him. He held himself with great pride and stature and most everyone in the school had a high amount of respect for him. Principal Ferguson had the undivided attention of the young men as he stood directly in front of them.

"First of all, I want to congratulate you on last night's comeback. I think you boys can do some good things here at Carver High in the next few years. However, I didn't call this meeting to pat you on the backs, rather I wanted to discuss your coaching situation. Thank goodness that Coach Jackson is going to be okay, but as you all know, he can't come back this year. Doctor's orders! Because of this, we recruited a new coach. Your new coach is out talking to the varsity players right now. Go on out and meet him." Rumors of Sleepy being at the school had reached all the players and they were all thinking, and hoping, the same thing.

The principal had to jump out of the way as the players bolted for the door. They ran onto the gym floor to see the whole varsity team standing in a circle around Sleepy Phillips. At once, all the guys let out a huge cheer and ran towards Sleepy. Sleepy turned his head and grinned as he saw his new team running towards him. Sleepy had heard millions of people scream for him before, but this felt better than any of those times. Sleepy excused himself from the varsity team. The varsity coach thanked Sleepy and told his team to start their lay-up drill.

"Okay guys, why don't we go sit in the bleachers and I'll explain," Sleepy said to his team. He sat in the middle of all nine boys and began to explain what had happened.

"Boys, I have to be honest with you," he started. "I miss the game of basketball very much. Ever since I retired, I've been sort of lost. Basketball is just a game to some people, but it has been my whole life. Ever since I was a little boy, I wanted to play basketball. However, my body won't let me play every day now, so I had to retire." The entire team was listening intently. Sleepy was a hero to these boys and they were hanging on his every word.

Sleepy continued, smiling now, "The other night during your game, I was getting that old feeling back, that feeling of competition. The feeling of wanting to play, to dive after loose balls, to win as a team. As I watched you boys doing it, I felt good that I was helping you, by coaching. The funny thing is, I think I enjoyed coaching as much as I did playing." Sleepy paused, looked at each of the boys and then continued on. "So, because you needed a coach and I needed a team, I decided to coach you guys the rest of the year." Sleepy looked at their faces. There were only smiles. "Okay then, it's set. We practice every day at five o'clock, directly after the varsity team finishes their practice. Don't be late and get a little something to eat beforehand." As the players were leaving, Sleepy's eyes fixed on Jimmy. Jimmy was smiling from ear to ear. Sleepy did not realize he was smiling the same way.

CHAPTER V

Back To The Basics

Jimmy listened to his teammates talk excitedly about their new coach as he laced up his hightops. Jimmy was quiet and fair, but a hard worker and a fierce competitor. This earned him the respect of his friends. His friends knew he was something special. Jimmy's immense athletic talent was obvious to everyone, but the way in which he handled himself drew them even closer to him. He was always in control, hard to anger, and never self-serving. Now, to top everything else, Jimmy had finagled the great Sleepy Phillips to coach their basketball team. Jimmy was a special person and the people around him were beginning to see this in full light.

Good news always travels fast, or so it seemed to Jimmy and the rest of his teammates. By the time their practice had started, there were about a hundred people in the stands waiting to watch. One of those people was an old sports reporter named Skits Cunningham. One of Skits' grandchildren attended Carver High and had called his grandfather, alerting him to this newsworthy event.

Someone else had called a television news program and they had sent out a reporter and a film crew. They were setting up their equipment in preparation for the six o'clock news.

Nobody had ever been to one of their practices before and the team found it quite interesting.

Jimmy spun around quickly, his eye catching on something. He chuckled as he watched Kenny being interviewed by the television reporter. Jimmy then laughed out loud as he watched Bull pull the reluctant Kenny away from the reporters.

"You had better focus on practice before Sleepy comes out here and sees you," Bull said to Kenny.

"You just don't know a star when you see one, muscle head," Kenny responded. Bull simply grabbed Kenny, threw him over his shoulder and walked away.

"I'll talk to you after practice," Kenny yelled from Bull's shoulders to the laughing reporter.

Principal Ferguson then came in through the gym doors with two security guards and walked to center court. He took a deep breath and started talking in a loud voice.

"Everybody, please leave," he started. "The team is trying to hold their first practice with their new coach and they can't do it with everybody creating a commotion. Sleepy has told me that he will be available to the media in the next couple of days to explain what's going on. So," and the principal looked straight at the news crews, "you boys will just have to wait for your story." Principal Ferguson motioned to the security guards who then started escorting people out of the gym. When the last person had left, Sleepy came walking out of locker room.

"They're all yours," Principal Ferguson said as he exited the gym, leaving Sleepy alone with his team.

"Sorry about the commotion, fellas," Sleepy said to the team. "Unfortunately, it will probably be this way for a couple of days. Fortunately, the media will lose interest in a few days and leave us alone. All right then, first things first. Everybody line up shoulder to shoulder under the far basket. The kids raced to the basket and lined up underneath.

"Very good," Sleepy called with a voice resembling that of a Marine drill sergeant. "That's the way I expect you to move at all times, with purpose and with speed." The boys were surprised at the seriousness of Sleepy's demeanor. "I would like each of you to tell me your name and a little about yourself, starting with you." Sleepy was pointing at Bull, who was the furthest to the left.

"My name is Theodore William McKinnon." All the other players chuckled when Bull said this. "Most guys just call me Bull," he added seriously. He then glanced menacingly at his teammates.

"Okay then, Bull it is," Sleepy said, realizing that everyone was afraid of Bull.

Next in line was Tommy Peterson. Tommy liked to pull his socks up all the way to his knees. Sleepy hadn't seen players wearing them that way since his first days in the NBA. Tommy told Sleepy that he wanted to play point guard.

Next up was Too Tall. "Everybody calls me Too Tall, but my real name is Kenneth Farkson." This also brought a chuckle from the team since no one ever called him Kenneth. Kenneth didn't really like the nickname, but he had gotten used to it.

"I've seen guys a lot taller than you, so if you don't mind, I'll just call you Kenneth," Sleepy said. This brought a big smile to Too Tall's face.

Kenny was standing next to Too Tall. "I'm Kenny James. I played point guard last night. I'm the fastest guy on the team and I want to handle the ball just like you." Sleepy liked this kid's guts, but he liked the hair even better. It must have come at least six inches from his head.

"You can learn to dribble the ball just as good as I can if you really want to. I'll even show you the drills to use, but it's going to take a lot of practice," Sleepy cautioned him.

"I'll do it," Kenny proclaimed boldly.

"Good attitude," Sleepy nodded. Kenny thrust his chest out and stood up straight.

Jimmy was next in line. "My full name is James Thomas Feen." Sleepy could see Jimmy was thinking about what to say next. After a few moments of silence Jimmy said, "That's all I really have to say."

"Smart boy," Sleepy thought to himself. "If you don't have anything to say, don't say anything at all." Sleepy had only known Jimmy for a few days, but he could tell the kid had real potential.

Jonesy was standing next to Jimmy. "My name is Edgar Jones, but I like to be called Jonesy." Junior Hernandez, Mark Abronovich, and Willie Stone rounded out the team. Sleepy started to dribble the ball he had been holding in his hands. He also began to pace back and forth as he addressed his new team.

"First of all, I want to congratulate you on a terrific win last night. Winners play hard, no matter what the situation and that is exactly what you young men did. You dove for loose balls, scrambled for rebounds and played like a team. However, with the talent you men have, you should've never been in a comeback situation."

"Now, with that being said," Sleepy continued, "the number one reason I'm here is to teach you how to play the game of basketball. There's a lot more to playing this game than shooting well or jumping high. It's called basketball savvy and that's what I'm going to teach you."

Sleepy was getting excited now. He was pumped up about becoming a coach and he put his real feelings behind his words. "One of the most important components of being a good player is conditioning. A good player plays tough defense, boxes out for rebounds, hustles for loose balls, sets picks and has court awareness. If you're tired, you can't perform to your ability. Your body will let you down. That won't happen to us; I guarantee it. Each man here will be able to play full-out for all thirty-two minutes of a game, or you won't be on the team." Sleepy stressed this last sentence.

This speech set the tone for the next two hours. Sleepy had the team running wind sprints and doing agility and defensive pressure drills. The pace was so tough that each of the boys had sweat dripping through his shirt.

Sleepy Phillips was not the kind of coach to sit around and watch. He laced his shoes tight for good reason. Before each drill he showed the kids what he wanted and how he wanted it done. He was constantly blowing the whistle, reminding his kids to "lose themselves in the game." He continually exhorted the players to push themselves harder.

After practice was over, each of the boys knew a few things they hadn't known before practice started. Number one was that Sleepy Phillips was still in shape. Number two was that he didn't play around. Number three was that defense wins and number four, Sleepy loved to blow his whistle.

Sleepy entered the locker room after practice to address the team. He simply said, "Good practice, same time tomorrow," before walking out the back door. The security guards helped him make his way to his car. The media people had waited the two hours until practice was over and were now trying to get Sleepy to stop and talk, but he walked right through them without saying a word.

"That man is tough," Bull said out loud.

"Yeah, but he really knows the game," Jimmy replied.

"Still in shape, too," Too Tall added. "I'll bet he could still beat Vince Carter one on one."

"I don't know about that," Kenny jumped in, "but I'll bet we'll be able to beat Olympic runners at the end of the year." Everybody nodded their heads at that. Sleepy had worn them all out this first practice.

The minute Sleepy sat down for dinner, Sandra Phillips knew that her husband had enjoyed himself that day.

"Tell me all about today's practice," she asked.

"I don't know where to start," Sleepy answered with a smile. "Practice was great. The kids were enthusiastic. I felt young again."

"Honey, you're only thirty-seven years old. You are still young."

"You know what I mean. It makes me feel like I used to before all the attention. It makes me remember when I would shoot by myself at night as a kid. It really brings back the memories."

Sandra was happy for her husband. She knew his celebrity status had begun to take its toll on him.

"Do you want to go down to the courts later tonight?" Jimmy yelled to Bull as he headed for his front door. Jimmy and Bull lived in the last two houses on the street. Jonesy, Kenny, Junior and Tommy had already gone into their homes up the street.

"Not tonight. I'm going to work out."

"Okay, but get some sleep. We've got a lot of work to do if we expect to have a good season," Jimmy said to his friend.

"Don't worry about that," Bull replied. "When Sleepy teaches you his moves, you'll be unstoppable and so will we."

"I don't know about all that. See you in the morning, buddy."

As Jimmy entered his house, he knew that his mother was still at work because all of the lights were out. First thing he did was head for the refrigerator. His mom always left dinner there when she worked the late shift. He heated it up in the microwave and ate quickly while watching Jeopardy. Jimmy then grabbed his ball and headed for the neighborhood basketball courts.

Jimmy knew that if he was going to be the best, he had to practice more than anybody else. So that was exactly what he tried to do. Dribbling the ball down the sidewalk, Jimmy didn't even notice the sun setting and the street lights flickering on and off. He was deep in thought. Over and over again he replayed in his mind what Sleepy had said at practice. Jimmy was determined to go to tomorrow's practice prepared.

When the morning came, Jimmy grabbed his jump rope and headed to the driveway. On most mornings he would do a thousand single jumps and two hundred double jumps. His legs would ache as he took his morning shower, but that was the goal. A long time ago Jimmy's father had told him always to earn his shower. It seemed like good advice.

After Jimmy's last class he met Bull, Kenny and Tommy at The Ice Cream Parlor for a soda. Two hours to kill before practice. It seemed more like twenty hours to these boys who were chomping at the bit to practice with their new coach.

The four friends grabbed their favorite booth and watched as the place filled up with students. Of course, everyone was talking about the same thing; the ninth grade basketball team and their famous coach.

Jimmy listened in on the conversation next to him. Two seniors were talking about how some ninth grade kid had bet Sleepy Phillips in a round of golf and had won. The senior was reading from a newspaper article.

"Anybody have a quarter?" Jimmy asked. Kenny handed him one. Jimmy went outside and bought a newspaper. Sure enough, the front page had Sleepy's picture and a story beneath it. The article was a little off base with the facts, but in general they had gotten the story right.

"We're going to be in the papers everyday," Kenny proclaimed happily.

"Don't go thinking that," Bull warned. "You heard what Sleepy said. Pretty soon they'll find another story and forget all about us."

"Bull's right," Jimmy said. "If anybody knows how the media acts, it's Sleepy." Still the boys had a good laugh at their newfound publicity.

Practice was very similar to the day before, grueling physical conditioning and lots of basketball strategy. The boys were coming to respect Sleepy greatly. He didn't lecture about life, he lectured about basketball. He said he was there to coach and that is what he did.

"The team that wants to win the most usually does, and you can always tell who wants to win the most. It's the team that sweats the hardest," Sleepy preached. Even though practice was tough, the players loved every minute of it and so did Sleepy.

———————

Jimmy walked in through his front door around 7:30 p.m. He was surprised to see his mother in the kitchen.

"You're home early, Mom. What's up?" Jimmy asked.

"They gave me the night off," Mrs. Feen replied as she stirred up the soup she had been making for dinner. "They said I deserved the night off and I agree with them." And with that she started laughing out loud.

Jimmy loved to see his mom laugh. He knew she was happy and in a good mood when she did. Too many times she put on a happy face, but inside he knew she was lonely or sad. This time, however, the laughter was for real.

"Are you hungry, baby?" she asked, and without waiting for an answer, filled up a large bowl and set it in front of Jimmy who had taken a seat at the table. That was one of the few rules that Jimmy's mother enforced. You had to eat at the table.

After they finished dinner, Mrs. Feen asked Jimmy how things were going with school and the basketball team. She had read about Sleepy Phillips in the paper, but she didn't bring it up. She was going to let her son talk about it on his own. As Jimmy began to tell her the whole story, she leaned back into her favorite couch and smiled. She always knew her son was headed for something special, she just didn't know it was coming so soon.

When Jimmy finished telling her about the team and their famous new coach, she gave him some advice. "You know Sleepy Phillips grew up in a poor neighborhood and he pulled himself out. So, whatever he says, you listen to him and listen close."

"I will," Jimmy answered honestly. "Do you mind if I go shoot some down at the courts?" he asked her as he saw Bull walking up the driveway.

"You know I don't mind, but be careful of all of those wanna-be gangsters running around. If anybody says anything to you, put your head down and run."

"I will," he said as he grabbed his basketball and sprinted for the door.

Mrs. Feen watched her boy run down the street and she could not have been more proud. As she lay down on the couch to read the paper again, she laughed as she came to the story of Sleepy Phillips and the Carver High ninth grade basketball team. She fell asleep thinking about her son.

CHAPTER VI

Team Ball

George Washington Carver High School was preoccupied with one subject Thursday, namely the Eagles' ninth grade basketball team. The student body was more interested in the ninth grade team than in the varsity, and with good reason. The world-famous Sleepy Phillips was coaching the ninth graders. Everyone had read the newspapers and knew the whole story. All of the students knew of Jimmy Feen and the bet. They also knew of the team's great comeback in Sleepy's first game as coach.

When Sleepy entered the locker room at 6:00 p.m., his players were already getting dressed. Sleepy used a door in the very back of the locker room because it came from the custodian's lounge. Sleepy had bought lunch for a few of the custodians in return for them not telling anybody, especially the media about his secret entry point.

"Boys," Sleepy said, "you know what I've been preaching in practice. Now all we have to do is go out there and sweat hard. Everything else will come along naturally because we've been working hard." Sleepy continued, "There's a big crowd with lots of reporters tonight. I know that I'm responsible and I apologize, but do the best you can to ignore them."

It seemed strange to Jimmy that Sleepy was always apologizing for the media being around. Sleepy didn't want them around, but the boys on the team felt differently. They felt like stars and they were loving it.

"Hurry up and get dressed and get out on the floor for warm-ups." Sleepy's instructions broke Jimmy's train of thought. The team hit the floor and started doing their lay-ups. Sleepy followed close behind and as he came into view, the cameras clicked, the lights flashed and the sold-out crowd erupted into a deafening cheer.

"Boy oh boy, I hope this doesn't last all year," Sleepy muttered to one of his security guards.

The Eagles came out raring to go. Sleepy started Jimmy, Too Tall, Bull, Kenny and Jonesy. Sleepy had the boys playing half-court man-to-man defense. Jimmy scored two quick lay-ups after stealing passes. The second steal had the crowd roaring its approval. Even Sleepy stood and cheered.

The man Jimmy was guarding had dribbled to his left, bounced the ball behind his back and tried to fake Jimmy out. Jimmy poked his left hand out and knocked the ball from his opponent's control. Jimmy then neatly sidestepped his opponent, grabbed the ball and dribbled the length of the court. Just as Sleepy had been teaching the players, Jimmy laid the ball cleanly off the backboard and into the basket. To everyone's amazement, including his own, Jimmy's hand was about a foot over the rim when he laid the ball against the backboard.

The game was a blowout with the Eagles leading 35-16 at halftime. Jimmy scored sixteen points, with Bull adding ten.

During halftime, Sleepy replaced all the starters, except for Jonesy. The second team did not miss a beat. The half-court man-to-man defense worked so well that Sleepy stopped using it, in order to not embarrass the other team. The final score ended at 61-41.

Sleepy only said a few words after the game. "Good game, good hustle, but we'll be playing better teams," he warned. "Tomorrow, I expect each of you to report directly to the library after school. Bring your books because we're going to do some studying." All the guys moaned and sang their disapproval.

Sleepy quickly quieted them down and told his team, "Anybody not making the grades won't play, period." The room went silent. The players did not expect to be scolded after a win. "However," Sleepy said as he broke into a smile, "I have a surprise, so it won't be so bad." With that, the music was turned up loud and the good natured ribbing associated with a winning locker room began.

The next day each of the team members was thinking about the surprise Sleepy had mentioned the night before. After their last classes, Kenny, Bull and Jimmy met up and headed for the library.

"I'll bet he's going to buy a bus for our away games. You know a man like Sleepy Phillips only travels in style," Kenny said as his imagination ran wild.

"No way, man. Sleepy isn't going to spend fifty thousand dollars on a bus," Bull replied hastily.

"Why not?" Kenny replied strongly, a bit perturbed that Bull rejected his idea. "Fifty thousand is chump change for Sleepy. He wouldn't even know it's gone."

Bull just rolled his eyes at Jimmy, who laughed. "I don't know what the surprise is, but I sure want to find out," Jimmy said, trying to relieve any tensions between his two friends. The boys walked into the library and saw the rest of the team sitting around one large table in the back corner.

"Yo, yo," Willie said loudly as he saw Jimmy, Bull and Kenny walk into the library. Jimmy felt embarrassed because everyone in the library had stopped what they were doing and looked at the team disapprovingly. Jimmy wished Willie had not spoken so loudly.

"What's up, Willie?" Jimmy replied quietly, shaking his hand.

"We're just waiting for Sleepy to show up and give us our surprise," he said loudly again. Jimmy looked around at the rest of his teammates. They were busy talking. Nobody was studying.

"What do you think the surprise is?" Jonesy asked Jimmy. Jimmy replied by shrugging his shoulders.

Sleepy had scouted out the library before school had ended. He did this to avoid being mobbed by the students. He surprised the entire team by entering the library through the back door, directly behind where they were sitting.

"Are you boys going to study or talk?" Sleepy asked in a hushed voice. Kenny, who had been talking about all the things Sleepy might buy, literally fell out of his chair as he turned to look. Sleepy had surprised them all. The rest of the boys just snapped their heads around in surprise.

"It sure doesn't look like you guys are studying," Sleepy playfully scolded them. "Now open some books and get to work. In one hour meet me in the locker room." As Sleepy walked out of the library, he waved to the librarians, who smiled back. He also stopped to sign an autograph for a student. Sleepy figured he could stop signing autographs pretty soon because everyone would have one.

"That sure was a long hour," Jimmy whispered to Junior Hernandez as the whole team rose from their seats and began collecting their belongings. Jimmy hardly ever studied. His mother insisted that he do his school work, but she worked so much at the hospital that she really couldn't enforce it. Despite his reluctance to study, Jimmy was not dumb. He was a silent, street-smart type who knew the difference between right and wrong. However, when it came to studying, Jimmy thought it was a waste of time to study things he was never going to use when he got older.

Sleepy had spent the last hour moving video equipment from his car to the locker room. He had paid a student to videotape the Eagles' last game and was now setting up the equipment so the team could watch a replay. When the boys walked into the locker room, they were surprised to see the video equipment.

"Sit down everyone," Sleepy started. "I taped our last game and we're going to review it now." Sleepy saw the look of disappointment on the faces of his players. "What's the problem?" he asked.

Jimmy was hoping that nobody would say anything. He felt awkward as it was. The team, himself included, had built up the surprise to be some expensive gift. But the fact was, Sleepy was concentrating on basketball and trying to teach them something. Jimmy felt ashamed that he had even thought about some sort of gift. Just then, Kenny stood up.

"Coach Phillips," Kenny started. "We were all hoping that the surprise would be...," but Bull quickly stood up and put his hand over Kenny's mouth and forced him to sit down by applying pressure to Kenny's shoulders. Jimmy breathed a sigh of relief.

"What Kenny was trying to say was that we all want to watch the game film, so let's get down to business," Bull said as he sat down next to Kenny, his hand still over his friend's mouth.

Jimmy voiced his approval and quickly got up and pushed the play button, trying to ease an uneasy situation. Sleepy broke into a smile as he realized what was going on.

"Okay, then," Sleepy said matter-of-factly, "let's get down to business."

Sleepy told the kids what he wanted them to look for and then explained by using the replay of the game. Jimmy made a mental note to tell his teammates they shouldn't expect any expensive gifts. Heck, they were just lucky enough to have Sleepy Phillips coaching their team.

As for Sleepy, he knew the kids were expecting something else. "Boys will be boys," he chuckled inside. Sleepy pointed out to his players why the pick-and-roll play didn't work sometimes, while it worked others. He made them concentrate on the positioning of the defensive player. He also showed them when their hands were down on defense and when they didn't box out for rebounds. Sleepy didn't let the team watch the video just for fun, he made them learn something.

"If we had played a better team, we might have lost," Sleepy told them, "but that's what practice is for." The team hit the playing floor after an hour of watching game films. Sleepy concentrated the whole practice on the pick-and-roll offensive play and boxing out for rebounds. He ran the boys very hard and there was not a single one that wasn't dripping with sweat.

Near the end of practice, Sleepy called the team to the center of the floor. "Number one," he started, "the hustle in the last game was good, but not great. You should give your last ounce of energy in every game. If you don't, then you're not playing as good as you could be."

Sleepy truly meant what he was saying and the boys could hear it in his voice. "I know a lot of you guys want to go to college and play basketball, but the only way anybody can make it is to hustle. If you hustle, your game will improve. If you're in better physical condition than your opponent, he's yours for the taking. When he's tired and you can still make all of your moves at full speed, you have him beat."

"Number two, I didn't like what I saw in the library today." Sleepy's voice had changed and the boys knew he was angry. "You guys were joking around, making noise and not getting anything done. That's rude to the other students who were trying to study. Not only that, but you're cheating yourselves. I don't have enough time to tell you about friends of mine that either lost money or were embarrassed because they were not educated. I want all of you to write your class schedules down on a piece of paper and give it to me Monday. If you forget, it will cost you a hundred laps. I'm going to do some investigating. Not only do I want to have the best-conditioned team, but I also want the smartest. Now give me fifty laps and hit the showers." Sleepy left the gym in a hurry to reaffirm his displeasure with his team's study habits.

"Boy, he was mad," Too Tall said as he watched Sleepy walk out of the gym. As the boys began their laps, each of them wondered how serious Sleepy was about checking with their teachers. Some worried more than others. Jimmy didn't say anything, but he knew that if Sleepy checked with his teachers, he was going to be in big trouble. After they hit the showers, the boys headed home for the weekend.

CHAPTER VII

Mystery Girl

Jimmy hurriedly washed his plate, then grabbed his ball. He said goodbye to his mom and then headed for the neighborhood basketball courts. Bull was going to meet him there, but Jimmy always tried to beat his friend. Of course, Bull tried to do the same so it usually came down to a foot race, with Jimmy's long stride winning out over Bull's slower, but powerful pace.

Jimmy considered these basketball courts his second home. The games were great, the players friendly and it was also safe. There was an unwritten rule around the neighborhood that you could not start trouble at the courts. Anybody that broke the rule would have to face down the whole neighborhood.

Jimmy and Bull shot baskets for a half an hour before anyone else showed up. Because they were younger, if they didn't get to play in the first game, they usually didn't get to play at all. Usually the older guys would ignore Jimmy and Bull, but today was different.

"Hey, it's the two superstars," old Fred Thomas said mockingly. Fred was thirty-nine years old and already had a full head of gray hair.

"Did you bring your superstar coach with you?" Bill Johnson added as he laced up his shoes. Jimmy and Bull both knew it was good-natured ribbing, so they took it in stride.

As soon as ten guys showed up, they began to play full court games. As more players arrived, some talked to Jimmy, some messed with him, but everybody knew him now. The games lasted until about 11:00 p.m., but Jimmy and Bull stayed after everyone else had left and played one-on-one. They knew this extra time would pay off in the long run.

Sleepy arrived at Carver High early Monday morning. He had already picked up the class schedules of his players and was headed to the classrooms to meet with their teachers. He was going find out what kind of students he had on his team. Sleepy knew the importance of a good education. He had seen many of his friends lose their jobs, and their pride, because of low social and educational skills. Sleepy wasn't going to let that happen to his kids. Sleepy laughed at that notion. He had been coaching less than one week and they were already "his" kids.

Sleepy met with Bull's and Kenny's teachers this day. What he found out was quite interesting. Kenny was the class clown. Bull was quiet, but a hard worker. Bull's teachers raved about his leadership possibilities. Sleepy knew that he had work to do with Kenny, but Bull seemed to be doing just fine.

It had been a tough Monday on Jimmy. It seemed that his classes lasted twice as long as usual. All day long he looked at the clock. He wasn't really listening to the teachers at all, he was thinking about jump shots and half-court defenses. If he could only go to school for basketball, he would be an "A" student Jimmy often thought. Finally, the last class bell rang. It was 2:30 p.m. and the game started at 6:00 p.m. There was just enough time to relax, grab a bite to eat, hit the gym for some practice shots and then head for the locker room.

The high school was built around a grassy area in the shape of a triangle. Tall oak trees gave shade and the many benches were used as lunch tables and gossip seats. Most of the students headed for this courtyard after school. Jimmy, Bull and Kenny joined the crowd. Jimmy arrived first and sat on a bench as he waited for his friends. He watched as the courtyard filled up with people. Many were laughing and joking and all were relieved that a long school day had ended. A couple of students even came up to him and wished him good luck for this night's game. Jimmy spotted Bull and Kenny and was about to stand up when someone tapped him on the shoulder.

"Aren't you Jimmy Feen?"

"Yes, yes I am," Jimmy stuttered. Before him stood the most beautiful girl he had ever seen.

"I just wanted to wish you good luck tonight," she said. Jimmy was speechless. He tried to say thank you, but he couldn't talk. He just muttered something that even he could not understand. The girl smiled inquisitively, shrugged her shoulders and then walked away. Bull and Kenny had spotted Jimmy by this time and had come close enough to hear the conversation between the pretty girl and Jimmy. Bull was laughing hysterically.

"Ladies and gentleman, the next Don Juan," Kenny proclaimed loudly.

"Aw, shut up you guys," Jimmy responded. As the boys walked up the street to McDonald's, Bull and Kenny continued to mess with Jimmy, but Jimmy didn't hear any of it. He was deep in thought about that beautiful girl.

The boys got back to the school about an hour later. Kenny went to the auditorium to watch drama practice. Bull had reserved computer time in the library. This left Jimmy all by himself, which was exactly what he wanted. Now he could start to concentrate on the game. He headed for the gym, stopping by the athletic department to pick up a ball. While Jimmy was shooting in the gym, camera men and newspaper reporters began to arrive.

"Hey kid, what's it like playing for Sleepy Phillips?" one of the reporters asked him.

"It's great," Jimmy answered while continuing to shoot. "He really knows the game and he's teaching us a lot."

"What's your name, son?"

"Jimmy Feen."

"You're the best player on Sleepy's team," the reporter said back to Jimmy.

"I don't know about that, mister, but with Sleepy teaching us, we're getting better every day." Jimmy liked this back-and-forth chatter, although he made certain to keep concentrating on his practice shots.

Sleepy's voice came booming into the gym from behind Jimmy. "Jimmy, get away from those guys. They'll make you shoot bad." Sleepy was smiling as he walked towards Jimmy and the reporters. "How are you fellas doing?" Sleepy asked the news people. Without answering his question and all at once, they started asking him questions. Many of these news people had followed Sleepy's career from his high school days in St. Louis, all the way to the professional ranks. Sleepy knew many of them by their first names.

"Hey guys, I'd love to answer questions now, but I don't have time." All the reporters protested, but in a friendly way. None of them wanted to be on Sleepy's bad list. "Come on Jimmy, it's time to suit up." Jimmy went running into the locker room with Sleepy close behind.

After all the players had come to the locker room, Sleepy began his pre-game talk. "Boys, if you go out there tonight and lose yourselves in the game, I know we can win. Forget about school, forget about your friends, just lose yourself in the game. Only think about being the quickest, sleekest, hardest man on the court. If you think like that, the other team will be scared of you." Sleepy had the boys on the edge of their seats.

"Remember, man-to-man defense. Dive after loose balls, roll to the basket after setting picks, and box out for rebounds. If you do all these things at a hundred percent, there's not a team out there that can beat you." And with that, Sleepy sent his team out to the floor for warm-ups. They were fired up, ready to give it all they had.

As Sleepy followed his team out to the floor, he could see the jam-packed stands and the television crews surrounding the floor. Only his bodyguards kept people from getting too close to him. It was a chaotic scene, but electrifying.

"This is the most excitement I've ever felt in a high school gymnasium," Sleepy overheard a sports reporter say into a camera. Sleepy shook his head, clearing it of all the distractions and began to focus on the game. He looked at the other end of the floor. The opposing team looked tall. Sleepy also noticed a couple of quick guards, but one boy stood out from the others. He appeared to be too old for high school, let alone the ninth grade team. Sleepy figured his team was going to have a tough game tonight. He knew from experience that boxing out for rebounds was key when playing a bigger team. Sleepy heard the game horn go off over the cheers of the crowd. The boys huddled around him.

"All right, men. Same starting five as last game. Jimmy, Bull, Kenneth, Kenny and Jonesy. These guys are big, so box out. If we don't box out, we won't win," Sleepy added for emphasis. "Remember, good spacing on offense and cut to the basket. If you get trapped, get the ball into the triangle and cut to the basket. Also, look for the pick-and-roll whenever possible." Sleepy always felt like he was giving too many last-minute instructions, but it was just the basics, so he kept reinforcing them.

All the boys put their hands in the middle. "ONE, TWO, THREE, GO EAGLES!" they shouted in unison. The two teams shook hands and set up for the opening tip. Jimmy ended up standing next to the older-looking boy. He outweighed Jimmy by forty pounds, but was about the same height. After sizing up the other team's players, Jimmy pointed at this large boy next to him and proclaimed quietly, but confidently to his teammates, "I got this guy." Too Tall out-jumped his man to the ball, tapping it to Kenny, who hit Jimmy with a perfect pass going to the basket. The older-looking boy was caught flat-footed. Jimmy easily laid the ball into the basket.

As the other team worked the ball down the court, Jimmy's man slowly, but deliberately, made his way underneath the basket. Jimmy fought him with his legs and forearms, but the boy had too much strength. The opposing point guard faked a pass to the middle, clearing Kenny out of the way, and then bounced a pass to Jimmy's man who was still under the basket. The boy turned and bullied his way into the lane, rolling the ball off his fingertips and into the rim. The force of his body colliding with Jimmy's sent Jimmy flying towards the wall. The referee told the boys to play on. Jimmy hurried to his feet and sprinted to the other end of the floor.

The whole first half went this way. The Eagles used their quickness against the other team's size and strength. Jimmy scored fifteen points, helping his team forge a 36-31 halftime lead. However, he had amassed three personal fouls trying to guard his opponent.

"Gentlemen, we have to change our strategy on defense," Sleepy began as he paced back and forth in front of the chalkboard. "Jimmy come here. Act like you're guarding me in the low post." Sleepy roughly established position, boxing Jimmy away from the hand at which he wanted to receive the ball. "The reason I can do this is because I'm so much stronger than you. However, if you move in front of me, it takes my strength away and it causes me problems because of your quickness." Sleepy was becoming animated now. Sweat was beginning to form on his brow.

"Bull, when Jimmy fronts his man, you need to be aware of a lob pass over his head. If and when this happens, you need to leave your man and try to steal the ball or establish position and contest the lay-up. Kenny, if Bull rotates to Jimmy's man, you have to rotate over and cut off the passing lane to Bull's man." Sleepy was explaining the basics of a rotating defense, a defense used by all NBA teams. The boys were listening intently and after Sleepy explained a second time using the blackboard, the boys hit the floor, ready for the second half.

The Eagles came out and played the second half as Sleepy had instructed. Jimmy worked extremely hard on defense, moving from behind to the front of his muscular opponent. The rest of the team helped guard against the lob pass by rotating and contesting the passing lanes. Sleepy urged them to push the ball up the floor quickly on offense and the strategy paid off. Their edge in speed and quickness enabled them to convert easy lay-ups. The opposing coach was forced to substitute in order to field a quicker team. The Eagles had forced their opponents to do away with their power game and play a more up-tempo style. This was to the Eagles' advantage.

Jimmy's offensive game began to show the dedication of his late night practices. He swished three, 3-pointers in the third quarter. However, it was his explosiveness to the basket that had the crowd buzzing. After hitting the outside shots, he faked another one and then gracefully slipped around his man. He planted both feet on the floor and jumped towards the basket, palming the ball in his large right hand. Despite being about twelve inches over the rim, Jimmy laid the ball gently in. As Sleepy watched Jimmy, memories of his idol, Dr. J., came to mind.

The Eagles opened a fifteen-point lead at the beginning of the fourth quarter, allowing Sleepy to empty his bench. Bull stayed in the game with the four substitutes. After the game, Sleepy quieted the boys down in the locker room. He congratulated them on their tough defense and relentless hustle. "I think you fellas lost yourselves in the game tonight and good things happened," Sleepy said with a satisfied smile. Sleepy also reminded them of practice the next day at 5:00 p.m. "Remember, hit the library right after school." As Sleepy slipped out the janitor's door, he heard the noise of the fans and reporters just outside the locker room door.

———————————

Mrs. Feen was waiting for her son in the living room when he walked through the door. "How was the game tonight?" she asked.

"Great, we won."

"Yes, I know. Bull's little brother Charles was already here talking about how your team is the best now that Sleepy Phillips is the coach. He also said you had a great game. Your practice must be paying off."

"It is, plus Sleepy is a great coach. He gets everybody to think of the team first. Playing hard is the most important thing to him."

"You listen to that man. He knows what he's talking about," Mrs. Feen instructed her son. Jimmy laughed. She told him that just about every day now.

"I do, Mom."

"I know you do, son, but I'm your mother, so I have to keep saying it." After dinner, Jimmy jumped rope and then headed to bed.

———————————

When Jimmy got up the next morning, his mom already had breakfast cooking and was reading the newspaper.

"It looks like little Charles was right. You did have a good game."

"Why do you say that?" Jimmy asked as he sat down in front of his egg sandwich.

"It's right here in the sports page. You guys are big news." She handed the paper to Jimmy. Sure enough, on the front page of the *St. Louis Times'* sports section was a picture of Sleepy Phillips on the sideline during last night's game. The article went on to explain that Sleepy's team had won its third straight game without any losses. At the end of the article, the paper mentioned that Jimmy was the star player.

"I wish they wouldn't write stuff like this," Jimmy said to his mom as he put the paper down. "They don't even mention the other guys. They played great too." Mrs. Feen loved her son's humility. He might not think he was the star, but the papers sure did.

CHAPTER VIII

Media Darlings

Skits Cunningham had worked for the *St. Louis Times* newspaper for thirty-three years. He started out by covering local high school sports. Eventually he moved up to cover professional sports. He was regarded as one of the best sports journalists in the state, if not the country.

For a sportswriter, developing good relationships with the athletes is very important. As a young reporter, Skits became friendly with one of St. Louis' local athletes, who just so happened to be one of the best prep athletes in the country, Harold "Sleepy" Phillips.

As Sleepy's star rose, so did Skits'. Sleepy would always grant Skits the best interviews. They had, in a sense, developed a professional friendship. However, Sleepy was still careful with his words.

Skits had been intrigued by Sleepy's decision to coach ever since his grandson had called him and told him about the situation. To Skits, however, it just didn't seem to be adding up. If someone of Sleepy's stature had wanted to coach, he would go straight to the pros. Skits could not put his finger on it yet, but he smelled an even bigger story. Skits decided to make a trip to George Washington Carver High and visit his grandson. "Maybe he would even run into Sleepy Phillips," he laughed to himself.

Sleepy Phillips came out of Professor Thomas' science class with a perplexed look on his face. He checked Willie's and Too Tall's names off his list. He had discovered that both were underachievers in the classroom. Not bad kids, their teachers said, just not motivated to learn. Even though Sleepy was a bit disappointed, he had not given up. "I'll give them some motivation," he said under his breath as he walked to the classroom of the next teacher he was to visit.

All day long, fellow students came up to Jimmy and offered their congratulations. People he had never met before started conversations with him. Most wanted to know about Sleepy, but that was all right with Jimmy. He never tired of talking about him.

The one person Jimmy did look for, he never saw. He hadn't seen that pretty girl since that first meeting. Everywhere he went, he made sure he scanned the entire area looking for her. He hadn't figured out what he was going to say, except that he was going to ask for her name.

All the recognition was not positive however. The varsity team had become jealous of the younger players. Even though the varsity players idolized Sleepy too, they still felt they should be getting more attention around school. The fans that were packing the bleachers for the ninth grade games left as soon as the game was over, leaving only a half full gym to watch the varsity game.

Jimmy, Bull, Kenny and the rest of the team met for practice on the side of the court at 5:00 p.m. The varsity team was walking off the court at the same time, heading for the locker room. Lucius Jackson was the varsity team's 6'10" center.

"You boys are becoming Hollywood stars," Lucius said to Jimmy and Bull. They looked his way, surprised that Lucius had even said anything to them. He had never said anything before. "If I was you two, I'd keep an eye on each other," he continued. Bull almost confronted him, but Jimmy grabbed his arm and calmed him down.

"Don't fall for that trash. He's just jealous. Don't let him get the best of you," Jimmy advised. Bull grudgingly walked away.

Sleepy came out of the locker room as the varsity team was going in. He stopped and talked to them for about five minutes. He congratulated them on their win last night and told them to keep working hard. Inside, each of the boys had wished Sleepy was coaching their team. Even though they showed some jealousy towards the ninth graders, the varsity players were still overwhelmed to be around Sleepy.

"Excellent game last night, fellas. You're making a lot of improvements in your knowledge and understanding of the game," Sleepy said as practice began. Sleepy was in a good mood. His team had given an excellent effort on defense during last night's game, exactly what he had been trying to teach them to do. He told them, "Keep this up and you're going to be the best team in the state." Sleepy had a knack for firing up his boys and he had just done it.

Sleepy capitalized on his team's adrenaline flow and held an energetic practice. Instead of slowing the pace down with new plays and new defenses, Sleepy showed the boys jumping drills and outlet passing. The boys were sweating hard. Near the end of practice, Sleepy told the team to do lay-ups. The boys broke into two lines and began to do text-book lay-ups. Sleepy stepped to the third set of bleachers, sat down and stretched out. He watched as the team continued their lay-ups.

No one had missed yet and the boys began counting how many in a row they were making. "Twenty, twenty-one, twenty-two," they counted.

Kenny was really feeling good about his game. He had played well last night and Sleepy's pre-practice speech had his energy level at full blast. When Kenny received his pass he was already at full speed. He took three quick dribbles and exploded towards the basket. He jumped off one leg and laid the ball off the backboard and into the basket. As he let the ball go, he slapped his hand against the backboard. A strong lay-up. This set the tone for the rest of the guys. Each boy tried to be more powerful than the last.

As Jimmy's turn came back around, he was beginning to feel anxious. His adrenaline was up just like everyone else's and he felt that maybe he could dunk. Jimmy received the pass, dribbled once, and then took two long strides towards the basket. He gripped the ball in his right hand as he jumped. He then raised his right hand as high as it could go and then slammed it towards the basket. The ball ricocheted off the back of the rim and bounced all the way back past half court. Jimmy came down disappointed.

"STOP, STOP, STOP," Sleepy yelled as he scrambled out of the bleachers. "You're high enough to dunk. Why don't you just do it?" he said forcefully to Jimmy. "Stretch your body. Imagine in your mind dunking the ball and then grip it and throw it down. The only reason you can't dunk is mental. Now accept the challenge and throw it down next time," he said aggressively.

Jimmy's ears were burning. Sleepy had singled him out in front of everybody. Nobody else could dunk either, Jimmy reminded himself. Heck, he was the closest yet. Jimmy was mad. "Nobody can talk to me that way," he thought to himself. "I don't care if he is Sleepy Phillips. It doesn't give him any right to embarrass me," Jimmy muttered under his breath. Jimmy watched as Willie messed around and threw the ball into the backboard like he was trying to dunk.

Jimmy was still fuming as he waited in line. He started to visualize what he was going to do. He planned on taking the ball with one hand, jumping off one foot and slamming the ball through hoop and then hanging on the rim to prove a point. Too Tall rebounded Junior's lay-in and passed the ball out to Jimmy.

Sleepy raised his voice, "Well, what are you going to do, dunk it or give up?" Jimmy grabbed the ball aggressively, dribbled twice and cut to the basket from the foul line extended. He jumped off his left foot and swung the ball back with his right hand. He rose and rose. Finally, when his head was almost even with the rim, Jimmy slammed the ball through the hoop with such force that the whole support started shaking. Jimmy hung onto the rim a few short seconds and then swung off. His teammates were yelling and whooping it up. As he jogged to the back of the line, Jimmy saw Sleepy wink. Jimmy then realized that Sleepy was only getting him psyched up. It had worked.

Jimmy received his next pass going toward the baseline. As he came to the baseline, he stopped quickly, pivoted and spun back towards the court and to the basket. He picked up his dribble as his momentum carried him to both feet. He jumped, reaching high with his right hand, the ball cradled firmly in it. As he rose to the basket, he quickly slammed the ball into the basket. Jimmy's teammates, Sleepy and Principal Ferguson, who had just walked into the gym, were left with their mouths open. The strength and quickness of the dunk had them awestruck. As the gym stood quiet, Jimmy landed and then looked around. He had even surprised himself.

"That's it. That's it," Sleepy said, breaking the silence. "Hit the showers. Excellent practice today." Sleepy was impressed by Jimmy as well as the whole team. They were working hard and he wanted to reward them by letting them go early. "Remember, we have an away game tomorrow. We play Templeton. Be at the bus at four o'clock," and with that, Sleepy shut down practice.

The Eagles easily beat Templeton, their first away opponent. The tough defense Sleepy had been teaching worked to full effect. Templeton had trouble bringing the ball up the floor and starting their plays. The Eagles were causing the opposing players to hurry, and in turn, to commit turnovers. Everything was clicking. When the offensive plays broke down, the Eagles resorted to the pick-and-roll play which reaped them a basket nearly every time. The boys had caught on to what Sleepy was preaching.

The next morning was a real surprise for the team. As each of the boys arrived for school, they were amazed to see signs and balloons placed all over the school congratulating them on their win. Every day, with every win, they were becoming more and more well-known. The local newspaper featured them on the front of the sports page again with another glowing article written by Skits Cunningham. Even *ESPN* had a small feature on the team and their famous coach during *SportsCenter.* Of course, the main story was about Sleepy's coaching career, but the boys still got to see themselves on television. It was a dream coming true.

Jimmy felt as if everyone in the entire school wanted to shake his hand. All day long students would come and talk to him about the team and, more often than not, about Sleepy Phillips. Jimmy didn't mind the attention, but he had really wanted to see that pretty girl again, rather than all the other well-wishers. She was nowhere to be found, however. Every time Jimmy thought about her, he kicked himself for not asking for her name.

Sleepy had also noticed the attention his team was getting. He knew when he took the job that he would draw attention to his new team, but he had figured the media would have lost interest by now. The reason was clear however, Sleepy knew. These kids were special and the media recognized this as well. As long as the team was undefeated, the media would continue to follow their season.

CHAPTER IX

Track Stars

Sleepy had set up a small desk in the corner of the locker room where he liked to sit and plan the day's practice. Today, however, he was reviewing his notes on each of his players' schoolwork, and he was becoming more and more angry. Sleepy had always thought being a coach was much more than just teaching kids how to play a game. A coach had the responsibility of impressing upon his players the virtues of hard work, courage and respect. As he continued looking at his notes, Sleepy decided to take these responsibilities more seriously.

Mark Abronovich and Bull McKinnon were the only excellent students on the team. Kenny was a class clown, but all of his teachers liked him and said that he put forth good effort. Willie Stone and Too Tall were average students. Their teachers didn't know them well because of their quiet demeanors in class. This left the last four on the team.

Tommy Peterson was what the teachers referred to as a "trouble student." He talked rudely to the teachers and always had a wisecrack for his fellow students. Tommy knew the way to the Dean's office very well. He had been there many times.

Junior Hernandez was similar to Tommy, although he made trouble with other students more than with the teachers.

Most of the other kids didn't like him very much. Jonesy was another story. His teachers were worried about him. They noticed that he always seemed fatigued, as if he didn't get enough sleep. Some of his teachers were very up-front with Sleepy. They thought Jonesy might be on drugs. Sleepy was going to keep a close eye on this situation.

Jimmy was the last team member on his note pad. Every teacher said the same thing about Jimmy. He was an exceptionally bright young man, but he didn't do his class work and never turned in homework assignments. Jimmy wasn't any trouble in class. He never showed disrespect for the school or the teachers, he just didn't pay much attention. The teachers all laughed that Jimmy was too busy dreaming about the NBA to worry about school.

Sleepy felt bad as he reread his notes on Jimmy's schoolwork. He felt very close to Jimmy even though he had known him only a short time. Jimmy was an exceptional athlete. Sleepy had already discovered this. More importantly though, Sleepy thought Jimmy was a good young man and not afraid to take charge when he had to. Sleepy knew this was a recipe for success. Sleepy looked up from his notepad and thought about the golf bet and these last few weeks of coaching. It had been a real boost for him, but now he was going to get serious. This was his team, and his boys, and from now on they weren't going to get away with any of this nonsense. These boys were going to make something of themselves and he meant to help, not hinder them. Sleepy looked down at his watch and saw that the boys were going to be there any minute. As they entered the locker room, Sleepy met them at the door.

"Hurry up and get dressed," he said with a stern voice. "We've got a lot of work to do today." After the players had dressed, Sleepy told them to take a seat around the blackboard. He then addressed his team. "When I started this coaching job," he began, "I told myself to be easy and have some fun. I didn't want to work you boys too hard. I wanted this to be a fun year." Sleepy made eye contact with every player as he paced back and forth in front of his team. He wasn't yelling or screaming, but the boys knew he was deadly serious. "However, now that I've spoken with your teachers, I see that you don't need a hall-of-fame basketball player coaching your team, you need a coach. So, I have decided to become exactly that, your coach."

The boys looked at one another. The good students wondered what this was all about. The bad ones knew exactly. Sleepy pointed to the blackboard. He had written all of the boys' names on it. Sleepy continued, "I've circled Jonesy's, Jimmy's, Tommy's and Junior's names. Simply said, you boys have unacceptable schoolwork. You have to improve or you're off the team." Sleepy said this with a rigid jaw and an ice cold stare.

Next, Sleepy pointed at Kenny's, Too Tall's, and Willie's names. "You boys are decent students, but you need to step it up and become better ones." Finally he pointed to Bull and Mark. This time his face lightened up and a smile crossed his lips. "You two know what it takes to be excellent students. The rest of your teammates are going to need your help." Sleepy then opened the locker room door and walked out.

"Who does he think he is?" Tommy jumped up and said to no one in particular. "He's just supposed to coach basketball, not be a study hall monitor."

"Sit down," Bull said as he laced up his shoes. "You're the fool that got yourself in this mess. If you would shut your mouth in class, you wouldn't have this problem. Sleepy is just trying to help and you're bad-mouthing him."

Tommy started to reply but stopped as he saw Jimmy get up and walk towards the gym door. "What do you think about this?" he asked Jimmy.

Jimmy stopped and turned around. "I think we'd better improve in school if we want to keep playing," he said before continuing out to the gym floor.

"Shoot, that man can make you work," Willie Stone muttered as he trudged into the locker room at almost 7:00 p.m.. The rest of the boys echoed these same thoughts as they slowly made their way in and sat down.

"I think he meant it when he said he was going to take this coaching job seriously," added Kenny, who for one of the only times in his life was too tired to joke.

Jimmy knew this had been the toughest practice yet. It seemed that Sleepy wanted to run them ragged, as if to prove a point. He had certainly done that, Jimmy realized as he slowly unlaced his shoes.

"Not so fast, Jimmy." Jimmy looked up, surprised to see Sleepy standing in the doorway. "I want to see you, Tommy, Junior and Jonesy down at the track," Sleepy said while looking straight at Jimmy. He then turned and walked out. Jimmy looked at Jonesy, Junior and Tommy and saw the exhausted looks on their faces. Now they wondered what else was in store for them. The rest of the guys in the locker room started giving them the business.

"We all know who the teacher's pets are, don't we?" Kenny laughed out loud.

"Yeah, I'll bet you four are going to get some sort of surprise," Too Tall added. All the boys laughed at this thought because each of them knew that Jimmy, Junior, Jonesy and Tommy were in for a physically exhausting running session. As Jimmy finished re-lacing his shoes, he heard someone laughing in the corner. He turned and saw it was Junior.

"What's wrong with you?" Jimmy asked.

When Junior had stopped laughing long enough to answer, he looked at all his teammates and said, "If I wasn't laughing, I'd be crying," he answered. After the four of them had left the locker room, the boys heard the rest of their teammates burst out in laughter.

Sleepy was standing at the base of the football bleachers with a stop watch in his hand. "Boys, I want to teach you a lesson," he said as they arrived. "School is not something you should take lightly. Ignorance shows and if you shrug off the responsibilities of your schoolwork, you will end up ignorant. I will not contribute to your ignorance. However, I'm not here to punish you, so you can leave anytime you'd like." All four boys stood their ground. They knew they were being tested and all four meant to meet the test.

"You young men are going to be with me, down here, two times each week. I'll talk to your teachers periodically to see if your attitude about school has changed. I hope it will." Sleepy knew this was the right thing to do. He had a feeling these boys would respond well to the challenge.

"First of all, give me twenty times up and down the stadium and then meet me at the track," Sleepy instructed them firmly. The boys loosened up a little, for they had tightened up a bit since practice had ended, and then headed up the stadium steps. When they reached the top they turned around and saw Sleepy on the football field below. He was lacing up his track shoes. After the boys completed their second sprint up the steps, they saw Sleeping begin to stretch his legs. While the boys continued their sprints up and down the bleachers, Sleepy began to jog slowly around the field. The boys couldn't help but to stare at him. His stride was graceful and strong.

"He's still in incredible shape," Junior said as he stared.

"Yeah, he looks like he could still dominate the NBA," Tommy replied. The boys continued towards their mark of twenty repetitions and as they did, Tommy told a story of a time that he saw Sleepy and his Minneapolis Blues play the New York Knicks. The boys were tired, but that didn't slow Tommy's enthusiasm as he remembered the game.

"One time, Sleepy got the ball on the left wing, took one dribble and jumped, well, he jumped sideways almost," Tommy tried to explain. "Then he hesitated in mid-air, pulled the ball back and slammed it home."

"I saw that," Jimmy said. "It was nasty."

"I saw it too," Junior added. "I think he scored forty-six that night."

"He did," Tommy shouted, excited that his friends knew exactly which game he was talking about.

The boys completed their repetitions just as Sleepy was putting his jogging suit back on. It had been a long practice and the stairs had taken the last of their energy.

"Okay guys, I know you're tired, but I'm serious about your study habits. School is the most important thing. I can't stress this enough." Sleepy was deadly serious as he said this. He looked at each boy individually until they looked him eye to eye. "Give me two laps and you can get out of here," Sleepy said as a smile crept across his face.

All four players began by running side by side. When they passed Sleepy to begin their second lap, Sleepy yelled at them to push themselves. "Give it all you've got," he shouted. They continued running together around the first turn and as they approached the second turn, Jimmy and Tommy began to pull away from Junior and Jonesy.

Jimmy and Tommy ran stride for stride down the backstretch with Tommy cutting in front of Jimmy on the third turn. Jimmy stutter-stepped so he would not fall and then began to shift into high gear in the outside lane. Sleepy watched in amazement as Jimmy's long legs began to eat up distance. At one hundred yards from the finish line, Jimmy began an all out sprint. He easily passed Tommy with fifty yards to go and cruised across the finish line.

Bull had waited in the library for his buddies to finish their sprints. As usual, the boys all walked home together. Junior and Tommy both headed straight for their beds when they reached their homes.

"I have an idea," Jimmy said as the rest of the guys continued the walk to their homes.

"Let me guess," Bull laughed. "You want to go play a couple games down at the courts."

"How'd you guess?" Jimmy asked.

"I know you can't stay away from the courts. How long have we been friends?" Bull answered as he, Jonesy and Kenny all laughed.

Jimmy and Bull held their own against the older players, but Jonesy and Kenny had trouble competing with their strength. The older players liked to tease these four ninth graders, but that was just a front. They actually thought highly of each of them.

Many people in the neighborhood thought Jimmy had the talent to play in the NBA one day, but they never talked that way around him. They were sure it would go to his head as it had to so many other players from their neighborhood.

After a couple of games, the boys decided to head home. It was already after 10:00 p.m. As they left, an older player continued to tease them, saying that if they wanted to stay on the court longer they should bring their superstar coach. All the other older guys laughed at this.

"I sure wish Sleepy would come down here and shut them up," Jimmy said to Bull as they were leaving.

"Yeah, me too, but pretty soon you'll be dunking on all of them and that'll shut them up," Bull stated with assurance. Jimmy, Bull, Jonesy and Kenny all went to their respective houses and ate a late dinner. Each fell asleep before his head even hit the pillow.

CHAPTER X

Behind Every Good Man Is A Good Woman

"Wake up son, you need some breakfast before you head to school," Mrs. Feen said gently through Jimmy's door.

"All right Mom, give me a minute." Mrs. Feen headed back for the kitchen and as she did, Bull, Kenny and Tommy Peterson came walking in through the front door.

"I'd better put on a few more pancakes with you wolves here," Mrs. Feen joked. She liked it when Jimmy's friends came over, even if she did have to feed them. She knew that a boy who had good friends was a very lucky one, and she was going to do whatever she could to make Jimmy's friends feel welcome. All the boys greeted her kindly and then headed directly for Jimmy's room where they barged right in and razzed him out of bed.

"Get up you lazy dog," Tommy joked as he shook Jimmy.

"Shoot, if my mom fixed breakfast for me, I'd be up and waiting," Kenny added.

Jimmy got up and jumped in and out of the shower. He sat down at the kitchen table just in time to get his portion of the scrambled eggs, sausages and pancakes. The boys ate all the food in less than ten minutes and then headed for the door.

"See you later, Mom," Jimmy said over his shoulder as he was leaving. The other boys thanked her for breakfast on their way out. When they were gone, Mrs. Feen sat down on the couch. She felt as if a hurricane had just swept through. After a few moments she headed for bed. She had gotten home at 2:30 the night before and was tired.

When the boys were only a few hundred yards from the school, Jonesy came running up from behind. "Hey guys," he said. "I've been busting it the whole way trying to catch you. I should do this every morning. It's a good workout."

"If you would get some sleep at night, you could have some of Mrs. Feen's breakfast and walk to school," Kenny said to him accusingly. Jimmy and Bull looked disapprovingly at Kenny. All the boys knew Jonesy had been having trouble at home. Sleep wasn't the easiest thing for him to get. Bull punched Kenny in the leg, giving him a charley horse, but Jonesy just ignored Kenny. Jonesy knew Kenny couldn't keep his mouth shut.

"Don't worry about it, buddy," Jimmy said to Jonesy as the boys walked onto the school grounds. Jonesy nodded his head.

The boys were surprised to see Sleepy sitting on the front steps of the school. A whole crowd of students had circled around him, and he was signing autographs, laughing and joking with them. When Sleepy saw the boys approaching, he excused himself from the crowd and walked over to his players.

"Hello boys," he said.

They all returned the greeting. Sleepy could tell they were surprised to see him this early. Before they could ask him why he was there, Sleepy told the guys that he needed to speak with Jimmy in private. Jonesy, Bull, Kenny and Tommy headed for class while Jimmy followed Sleepy, who had started to walk around the main building.

"Don't worry about your first period class," Sleepy said to Jimmy. "I already talked to your teacher. I told her you would be a little late." Sleepy looked at Jimmy in a way that made Jimmy feel as if Sleepy was about to break some bad news.

"What's up, Coach?" Jimmy asked. By this time they had reached the gymnasium. They went inside.

"Sit down and relax," Sleepy instructed his star player. Sleepy looked at this fifteen year-old kid and smiled. "You remind me of myself sometimes, Jimmy, although you're better with the golf clubs." Jimmy smiled uneasily, still unsure why Sleepy was talking to him right now.

"You know, when I was your age they kicked me off the basketball team because of my grades," Sleepy said. Jimmy knew that already. Every kid in America knew the story of Sleepy Phillips. Sleepy continued, "Well, I wanted to play basketball so bad that I wouldn't let anything get in my way. I decided to get serious about my schoolwork. Funny thing happened too. I became interested in learning. Not always what the teacher was teaching," Sleepy laughed, "but in what the teacher could teach. On my own, I learned about the space program, the natural resources of the Earth and the resources of my own body."

Sleepy was getting excited. Jimmy could tell by the way his voice rose a level. "Simply said, I decided to know about the world. I decided to be intelligent. I know sometimes it's not easy to study. Some people think it's nerdy, but if you ever want to rise above and realize your dreams, you've got to know what's going on. The only way to do that is to listen, read and think for yourself."

Jimmy started to say something, but Sleepy cut him off. "Jimmy, to be quite honest with you, your grades and effort in school is not up to the level that I will accept. However, I'm going to give you another chance." Jimmy looked at Sleepy inquisitively.

"What do you mean?" Jimmy asked.

Sleepy looked at him with a big smile. "I'll make you another bet." Sleepy paused, allowing this to sink in with Jimmy. "If you don't make a 3.0 this semester, you attend summer school. Three classes all summer long and you take what I pick for you."

"And what if I win?" Jimmy asked confidently.

"Name your price."

Suddenly Jimmy had an idea. "If I win the bet, you come down to my neighborhood basketball court and play some pick-up ball." Sleepy weighed the offer silently. "Well, what do you think?" Jimmy asked with a sly smile.

Sleepy patted Jimmy on the shoulder. "I'll take the bet," he laughed. The superstar coach and his star player shook hands. "Okay, now get to class." Sleepy watched as Jimmy ran back towards the main building of the school. Sleepy had grown to like this kid. Jimmy wasn't a blowhard or a trash talker. All the other boys on the team seemed to look to him for leadership. Sleepy was hoping that Jimmy would win the bet.

Throughout the day, Sleepy surprised his players who had poor study habits. He challenged them much the same way he did Jimmy, although he didn't make any more bets. He was especially tough on Tommy Peterson, who not only had bad study habits, but also showed disrespect for his teachers.

Sleepy told Tommy to change his behavior immediately or be kicked off the team.

The day's practice went better than usual. The kids played hard and started to show the team play that Sleepy was striving for. The pick-and-rolls came naturally and the defensive rotation was becoming second nature. Sleepy was impressed by how well these kids were responding to basketball basics.

As the boys ran up and down the floor in a scrimmage, Sleepy kept a close eye on Jonesy. If there was drug use going on, Sleepy meant to do something about it. However, Sleepy wasn't convinced this was the problem. Jonesy did look a little tired, but he always practiced hard and was well mannered. Sleepy hadn't figured out how to handle this situation yet.

"That's it," Sleepy said loudly, interrupting the scrimmage. The boys all stopped and looked questioningly at Sleepy. Practice was not slated to end for another thirty minutes. "That's it. We're going home early tonight. Now stay out of trouble this weekend and I'll see you on Monday." Sleepy turned back towards the team just as he was about to leave, "By the way, my little group is still meeting at the track." Jimmy, Tommy, Junior and Jonesy looked at each other and groaned.

Jimmy arose very early Saturday morning. He was scheduled to caddy at the golf course for the first time since he had won the bet with Sleepy. He arrived before any of the other caddies or golfers showed up.

"Hey there, superstar," Tony Mendez said as he saw Jimmy walk into the equipment room.

"I'm no superstar," Jimmy replied to his boss. "Sleepy's the superstar. If it wasn't for him, our team would be just any old ninth grade team."

"You might be right about that, kid, but you guys are undefeated and the papers are saying you might stay that way for the rest of the year."

"I hope they're right," Jimmy said as he held one of the practice clubs. "Sleepy sure is a good coach. He's really teaching us how to play the game. I think we're going to make a good team someday."

"I think so too," Tony agreed. He had been to one of the games and was impressed by Carver High's play.

"Tony, do you mind if I hit some practice balls before everybody gets here?"

"No problem kid. You know where everything is. Help yourself." Jimmy did just that. As soon as the first two golfers arrived, Tony assigned Jimmy to them. Jimmy carried both bags by himself.

"Fifty bucks, not bad," Jimmy thought to himself as he headed home from the golf course. The golfers had recognized Jimmy from the pictures in the newspapers. They asked him a bunch of questions about Sleepy Phillips and the team. Jimmy guessed that was the reason the tip was so good. When he walked through his front door, his mom had lunch waiting. Jimmy glanced at the clock on the wall as he sat down and saw that if he ate fast, he could be one of the first players to the basketball courts. "No time to waste," he thought as he inhaled his food.

"Slow down, son, the basket is still going to be there when you get done. If you eat that fast, you aren't going to be any good anyway," his mother said, admonishing him. Jimmy knew she was right, but he was almost done. After he finished, he called Bull and Kenny and told them to meet him out front in fifteen minutes. He laced up his shoes and headed for the door.

"Wait a second, Jimmy."

"Yeah Mom?"

"Be home tonight by five o'clock. We're going shopping." Jimmy's face dropped. "You don't have to go," Mrs. Feen said. She knew her son well and had expected this reaction. "I was going to buy you some new basketball shoes, but if you don't want them, we can just forget..." Jimmy stopped her in mid-sentence.

"Thanks Mom. I'll definitely be home," he said with a smile. His mother kissed him on the cheek before he headed out the front door to meet up with his friends.

———————————

Sandra Phillips was a loving wife to her husband. She was not only Sleepy's one true love, but also his best friend. She had not seen her husband so motivated in a long while. Since he had retired from the NBA, he had longed for a challenge. She knew he was bored. He didn't have to say it.

This had all changed in the last few weeks however, and she knew most of it had to do with a fifteen year-old boy named Jimmy Feen. "You should see this kid play, Sandra," Sleepy would tell his wife excitedly. "His athletic instincts are unbelievable. Quick like a cat and a body that will grow strong as he gets older." Knowing her husband as she did, she knew that Jimmy's athletic ability was not the sole cause for all of her husband's enthusiasm. Sandra wanted to meet Jimmy. As a matter of fact, she wanted to meet the whole team. However, all she ever said was, "Baby, maybe coaching is what you should be doing." Sleepy would always think about this and then respond with, "Maybe so."

———————

Early Monday morning, as Jimmy and the gang walked to school, the conversation focused on the upcoming week's basketball schedule. They had two games scheduled and if they won both, their record would rise to five wins and zero losses. Tommy changed the subject from basketball to girls.

"Hey, Jimmy, I saw that girl you've been talking about. She was at The Ice Cream Parlor. She asked about you."

Jimmy looked at Tommy, barely able to conceal his interest. "What'd she say?" he asked.

"She asked how you were doing," Tommy said smugly.

"What did you tell her?" Jimmy asked, too excited to see the trap Tommy was laying for him.

"I told her you would be doing better if she would just leave you alone."

Jimmy started to say something, but stopped himself when he saw all of his friends laughing. Tommy was playing a joke on him and he had almost taken the bait. "You didn't even see her, did you?" Jimmy asked.

"No, buddy, I'm just fooling with you," Tommy managed to say between his laughs. Jimmy took off toward Tommy, chasing him the rest of the way to school. All the boys were laughing, even Jimmy.

Sleepy was also up early Monday morning. A friend had called him late Sunday night with an idea for a ninth grade basketball tournament. Sleepy liked the idea and decided to go to the School Board for some information. Before he left the house, Sandra suggested that it would be a good idea to have the team and their parents over to the house for lunch one afternoon.

"That's a great idea, but we'll have to get more security so the kids don't tear the house down," he joked as he left.

Everyone at Carver High knew the story of Sleepy Phillips and his recent call to coaching. Because most of the students were following the team closely, Jimmy and his teammates had become celebrities around school. As Jimmy walked into the lunchroom with his tray of food, he was surprised to see most of his teammates crowded around one booth. Jimmy walked up behind the group to see what was going on.

"I'll bet you can't eat all that in one bite," Bull said to Too Tall.

"You wanna bet," Too Tall answered, issuing a further challenge.

Jimmy was confused. "What's going on, fellas?" he asked.

"Too Tall thinks he can eat a whole slice of pizza in one bite and then take a drink of soda. Bull doesn't believe he can do it," Mark answered, filling Jimmy in.

Too Tall had a habit of eating his food fast and in large quantities. He liked to show this strange ability to anyone who would watch. Too Tall proceeded to stuff the whole slice in his mouth and then take a drink of soda.

"I knew I shouldn't have bet. I think you suckered me," Bull said, mocking anger while putting a dollar into Too Tall's hand. Jimmy was about to sit down and eat when he felt a tap on his shoulder. He turned around and was surprised to see his mystery girl.

"You guys look like you're in a deep intellectual discussion. Maybe I should come back another time," she joked.

"No, no," Jimmy answered. "I was just sitting down to eat. As a matter of fact, I was going to find an empty table. There's too much noise here for me. Would you like to join me?"

"That would be great," she answered with a smile. Jimmy walked to one of the booths in the corner. He was nervous and looked back to see if his friends were watching. They were. The mystery girl followed him.

"First of all, what is your name?" Jimmy asked after they had sat down.

"Kim Williams."

"I sure wish I had asked you that the first time we met. Sorry I didn't, but I was a little tongue tied," Jimmy said with an embarrassed smile. The two teenagers hit it off right away. Lunch was over before they knew it, so they decided to meet after school.

"Where do you want to meet?" she asked.

"How about the library," Jimmy answered, remembering his bet with Sleepy. Kim nodded approvingly.

After Kim had walked out of the lunch room, Jimmy turned towards his teammates. He saw Kenny and Tommy acting like himself and Kim.

"I'll see you in the library," Kenny said to Tommy, imitating a high, female voice.

"We'll study poetry together, my love. No, wait, I can't leave you like this, kiss me," Tommy replied dramatically, mocking Jimmy's voice. Everybody cracked up.

"You'd think you two didn't have anything better to do," Jimmy said, feigning disgust.

"Don't feel bad, lover boy, we're just jealous," Willie assured Jimmy as he playfully rubbed Jimmy's head.

As the ninth grade team strolled out of the lunch room, laughing and generally making a scene, a few of the varsity team members were sitting and watching. They were getting more steamed by the minute. They were jealous of the attention the younger guys were getting.

"I'd like to get those young punks on the floor one day," Lucius Jackson, the varsity center, said to Brian Green. Brian was a forward on the varsity team.

"Yeah, me too. They have to be knocked down a notch," he said in agreement.

Sleepy walked out of the School Board's offices happy. Everything had gone as smoothly as he could have hoped for. Sleepy hadn't even thought about a ninth grade tournament until last night, and now it was a real happening. Sleepy was looking forward to seeing the faces of his players when he told them. He knew they would be surprised.

Sleepy looked at his watch and saw that he had a few hours to kill before practice, so he decided to play a round of golf. As Sleepy drove to the course, he started to plan the details for his ninth grade tournament. Sleepy knew it was going to cost him some money, but he had enough of that, and besides, these kids were good kids. Sleepy turned up the radio, stepped on the gas and headed for the golf course.

———————————

Jimmy arrived at the library first and decided to wait outside the front door for Kim. While he waited, a few of his fellow students came to him and wished him good luck. Jimmy thanked them politely, but when he saw Kim, he quickly excused himself.

"Talking to a few of your fans, I see," Kim teased him.

"You know the real reason they talk to me, don't you?" Jimmy replied.

Kim looked puzzled. "I'm not sure what you mean."

"If Sleepy Phillips wasn't our coach, nobody would care about any of us guys on the team."

"You might be right," Kim answered, surprising Jimmy with her honesty. He followed her into the library.

CHAPTER XI

Leaving It On The Floor

Monday's practice was a difficult one. Sleepy had the team concentrate on fast-break defense and outlet passing. These drills required a lot of quick bursts of speed and sudden stops. The boys hustled hard, but they did tire. Sleepy continually preached to the boys to "leave everything on the court." Sleepy was obviously focused for this practice. He was running up and down the floor blowing his whistle. "I want you to give the game everything you've got. If you practice your hardest, then you'll play your best," he was yelling to his players as they performed the drills.

When Sleepy finally stopped practice, he called all the boys to the center of the floor. "I have a surprise for you," he said. "You've been playing some good basketball, but you haven't played the best competition yet. Even though we're doing well right now, we don't know how good we are." The boys looked at each other with questioning glances. They didn't know what Sleepy was getting at. "So, along those lines," Sleepy continued, "I've entered our team into a season-ending tournament. The tournament will start approximately one week after our last scheduled game." Sleepy stopped pacing. He looked around at his players.

"What other teams are going to be in it?" Junior asked.

"All the best ninth grade teams in Missouri," Sleepy answered.

"Where is it being held?" Mark Abronovich inquired.

"Downtown St. Louis, in the Arena." There were no more questions. The boys seemed excited, but Sleepy wasn't sure. "The teams we'll play against will have records as good as ours. We will get a good indication of how good we really are." As he said this, Sleepy realized what was wrong with his team. They were a bit apprehensive about playing the best teams in the state. Sleepy decided to pump them up so practice would not end on a downhill note. Sleepy started pacing again, and the boys were watching him intently.

"It's true," Sleepy said, "we will be playing the best teams in the state, but we're ready," he stated confidently. "I've been around the best basketball players in the world. I know basketball as well as anyone and I see the talent on this team. You boys may not know it yet, but this is a special group. You have talent, basketball savvy and most important of all, you have heart. You have hearts big enough to leave everything on the floor and lose yourselves in the game. You have hearts big enough to sweat harder each time out. You boys play team ball, you find the open man, you box out and dive for loose balls." Sleepy was hyped up now and so were his boys.

The apprehension was gone and the straightforward, cocky nature of the team was back. Sleepy continued, "But not only do you have the heart, but you also have the talent. We're the best team and we're going to show everyone in that tournament what kind of damage the Carver Eagles can administer." Sleepy had started to break a sweat by this time. "Boys, let's do some lay-ups and I think I'll join you," he said.

The boys all had their adrenaline flowing and each tried to jump the highest they had ever gone. The excitement level was even higher since Sleepy was doing lay-ups drills with them. Even though Sleepy had been around them for a few weeks, they were still in awe. As Sleepy warmed up, he began to glide to the basket, using his left and right hands to dunk the ball through the hoop.

This was the first time the boys had seen Sleepy playing hard. Even though it was only a simple lay-up drill, they could see why Sleepy was the boss on any basketball court he stepped on.

After fifteen minutes of lay-ups, Sleepy told the boys to hit the showers. "All except for my track members," Sleepy deadpanned. The four boys he referred to did not see the humor. Sleepy had Jimmy, Tommy, Junior and Jonesy do the same routine as the other days. Again, the boys were spent after they had finished. The long days at school, practice, and the extra running was starting to catch up with them. Sleepy could see it in their faces.

"I hope your grades are better. I would hate to think that you want to continue this," he said as the boys were bent over at the waist, panting like tired dogs. "I'll be checking with your teachers at the end of the week, so keep studying," Sleepy warned. "Jimmy, I need to speak with you in private, please." Jimmy followed Sleepy over to the football bleachers. Sleepy stretched his long frame out on the first row of bleachers. Jimmy did likewise.

"I'm not sure how to handle this, so I guess I'll just talk straight up," Sleepy said.

"Okay," Jimmy answered, unsure where the conversation was heading.

"This is about Jonesy. Some of his teachers told me that he seems tired and withdrawn. They suspect he is involved with drugs. These teachers said they know his older brother is caught up in drugs and they fear the same thing is happening to Jonesy."

Jimmy was surprised that Sleepy knew this much about Jonesy. Jimmy did know that Jonesy's older brother was involved with drugs. The word around the neighborhood was that he was selling now, but Jimmy didn't think that Jonesy was in on it. Sleepy was staring at Jimmy now, waiting for a response.

"What do you think?" Sleepy finally asked.

"I'm not sure, Coach," Jimmy said. He didn't want to tell Sleepy anything that Jonesy didn't want him to. Jimmy and Jonesy had been good friends for a long time and Jimmy had learned long ago that friends have to stick together. He wanted to speak with Jonesy before he said anything.

Sleepy nodded understandingly. "See you tomorrow, Jimmy."

Jimmy trotted up through the gates surrounding the football stadium, past the outdoor basketball courts and headed towards the library where Bull, Junior, Kenny, Tommy, and Jonesy were waiting for him.

"What was that all about?" a very interested Tommy asked Jimmy.

"I'll tell you later," Jimmy said as he started walking home. Bull could tell that Jimmy was still thinking about what Sleepy had said to him. As the boys walked home, the usual chatter was not there. Each of the boys knew Jimmy was thinking about something serious. It put them all in a somber mood.

After Junior, Kenny, Tommy and Jonesy headed for their homes, Bull and Jimmy continued on down through the neighborhood. Bull asked Jimmy if he felt like going to the courts. Jimmy surprised Bull by saying no.

"I have to take care of a couple things," Jimmy said to Bull as he turned up into his driveway.

"Are you all right?" Bull asked him.

"No problem. I'll see you in the morning."

Bull knew Jimmy was lying to him, but he also knew that if Jimmy needed any help, he would ask. Jimmy headed straight for the kitchen. His mother was working the late shift tonight, but as always, she had left some food in the refrigerator. Jimmy ate, took a shower, and then headed for Jonesy's house.

Jimmy didn't like to walk on Jonesy's street after dark, or even in the daytime for that matter. It was only two streets over from Jimmy's, but there was a big difference. People living on Jimmy's street fought the drugs and the violence. Even though they weren't always successful, they tried to keep trouble off their street.

Jonesy's section of the neighborhood was different. Some of the houses were abandoned and the gangs used them to sell drugs. It was a dangerous neighborhood and Jimmy knew to keep his head down, mouth shut and feet ready to move. He reached Jonesy's house and knocked on the door. He could hear loud music inside, so he knocked again.

"What do you want?" Jonesy's older brother, Ted, shouted before he had even fully opened the door. When he realized it was Jimmy, he invited him in. "Jonesy is in his room," Ted said as he pointed to a door down the hall. Jimmy made his way to Jonesy's room, although he had to step around six people sitting on the floor of the living room. They were obviously high and dealing drugs. It made Jimmy extremely nervous even to be there.

"Hey, Jimmy, what are you doing here?" Jonesy said as Jimmy opened his door. "What's up?"

"Well, I got to talk to you. You mind if we walk a little bit and get out of this noise." They could barely hear one another over the music coming from the living room.

"Not at all," Jonesy replied. After they had walked outside, Jimmy told Jonesy about Sleepy's concerns. Jimmy was straightforward with the talk about drug use. Jonesy became upset, not at Jimmy, just angry that this was even being talked about.

"Man, you know I don't use that stuff. How long have you known me? You know I don't use that stuff," he repeated himself. "I've seen what it does to people."

"I know," Jimmy said apologetically, "but I had to ask. There are some people worried about you." Jonesy was staring blankly at the sky.

"Coach Phillips is right," Jonesy said. "I am tired. I can't get any sleep in that house. Ted doesn't give a damn about nobody but his freak friends and getting high. Man, I'm sick and tired of living like this. Addicts at the house all the time. The place is always dirty, but what can I do until I go to college?"

Jimmy listened sympathetically to his friend. He could tell Jonesy was hurting inside. Jonesy felt like he had no options. Suddenly, Jimmy had an idea.

"Why don't you stay at my house tonight?" Jimmy asked him. "You need some sleep. You said so yourself, and in the morning we can figure out what to do. Plus, we have a big game tomorrow and we can't afford to have you tired." Jonesy thanked Jimmy and accepted the invitation.

The boys walked to Jimmy's house without saying a word to each other. They didn't need to. Jimmy was very relieved that Jonesy was not doing drugs. He knew Jonesy was telling the truth. However, Jimmy was concerned about Jonesy's brother, Ted. Once they arrived at Jimmy's house, Jimmy grabbed Jonesy a spare sheet and pillow from the closet and told him to use the spare bedroom. "It's small, but the bed is soft," Jimmy said warmly.

Jimmy and Jonesy woke up the next morning at 6:00 a.m. Mrs. Feen already had breakfast on the table and soon thereafter, Bull, Tommy and Kenny came in through the Feen's front door. As the boys all ate their breakfast, Bull started asking Jimmy about Kim. Jimmy's mom acted like she didn't hear the conversation, but she hadn't missed a word. She was surprised because Jimmy hadn't said anything to her about this girl.

Jimmy quickly changed the subject to the game later that evening. The rest of the boys got the hint that Jimmy didn't want to have an open discussion about Kim. The boys finished their food, cleaned up and then headed for school. Jonesy hurried home to clean up and then raced to catch up with his buddies.

Game days were especially tough for Jimmy because he would daydream all day long. This, coupled with the fact that he looked at the clock every five minutes, made the game seem like a year away. Today was no different, although he did try harder to pay attention to his teachers. Jimmy still thought it was a little boring, but he wanted to win that bet with Sleepy. He couldn't wait to see the looks on the faces of the neighborhood players when he walked onto the courts with the greatest player of all time.

The boys met for lunch at the same time, at the same table. None of them were surprised to see Kim walk up. However, they were surprised that she brought three friends with her. When the fellas saw Kim's friends they all tried to be smooth. Kenny and Jonesy quickly made room for the girls to sit down.

"We just wanted to wish you guys good luck tonight. These are my friends, Kelly, Lisa and Amanda. We brought some presents for you," Kim said to all of the players. The four girls opened up a box and pulled out decorated bags filled with candy, cards, and flowers. The guys were stunned, while the girls left as quickly as they appeared. Kim stayed long enough to ask Jimmy if they would see each other after school. Jimmy said he would meet her outside of the library again.

As soon as the girls left, the young men began to examine the contents of their gifts. There were Snickers, M&M's and Hershey's Kisses, among other treats. The girls had obviously gone out of their way to make a very nice gesture. Between bites, the teammates began to wonder out loud which girl liked which boy.

"The tall one definitely had it going on for me," Kenny said seriously as he pulled out his comb.

"Come on, she couldn't even kiss you without giving you a stepladder. Everybody knows she was looking at me," Too Tall rebutted proudly.

"Argue all day long, Casanovas, but Kelly is fine," Junior said, "and she's all mine." The boys all laughed at his rhyme and the way he stretched out the words "fine" and "mine" with his voice. Jimmy was listening to the conversation and he began to get angry.

"We have a game tonight and we're eating chocolates like hogs and worrying about who likes who," Jimmy said with an unconcealed amount of disgust. "If we don't start thinking about what we need to do on the floor tonight, nobody is going to bring us anything tomorrow." His teammates knew he was right. They finished their lunches in silence, each thinking about that night's game. But like all young men, the girls were still in the back of their minds.

Kim and Jimmy met in the library after school. They studied for thirty minutes and then walked across the small campus to the cafeteria. Jimmy ordered a turkey sandwich and some fruit for his pre-game snack. While Jimmy ate, he and Kim talked about a variety of subjects, including school, their hobbies, and their friends. Basically, they talked about whatever came into their minds. The conversation was free and easy and both enjoyed it. After a while, Jimmy looked at the clock and saw it was time to head for the locker room.

"I'll see you at the game tonight, right?" Jimmy asked Kim.

"Definitely. I was hoping we could watch the varsity game together," she said inquiringly.

"Yeah, good," Jimmy said a bit apprehensively. He usually watched the varsity game with his teammates. Then an idea popped into his head. "Maybe you could get some of your friends, too. We could all watch the game as a big group." He knew if his teammates were worrying about which girl they liked, they would not have time to hassle him. Jimmy and Kim decided to meet outside the locker room after the game.

Jimmy met Bull in the locker room and the two of them hurriedly dressed into their uniforms and headed for the floor. Both boys liked to shoot practice shots before the game in order to start off hot. Also, even though neither one would admit it, they liked the back and forth conversations with the media people who were setting up to cover the game. One by one, the other players showed up on the floor. Thirty minutes before tip-off, Sleepy called his players back into the locker room.

Sleepy looked around at his team. Most of the boys were sitting by their lockers either stretching their legs or tightening their shoestrings. There was a serious nature about them and Sleepy liked it. "Men, you know what you have to do out there. You have to play hard, hustle and give it everything you've got. However, the most important thing you have to do is remember that when you're on the floor, you are a five-man unit. Pass the ball to a teammate for a better shot. Box someone else's man off the boards so your teammate can get the rebound. Remember, a team doesn't care who gets the glory. All a team cares about is getting the job done."

Sleepy was not raising his voice. He was talking matter-of-factly to the boys. "You know what you have to do, so go do it," he finished. The team walked out onto the floor and began their pre-game drills with a quiet efficiency.

By looking around the gym, most people would have thought a State Championship was being played. Cheerleaders had hung banners all over the gym walls and were doing cheers on the sidelines. Media tables were set up all over the gym with reporters doing spots for the evening news. People in the stands were buzzing about the world-famous Sleepy Phillips and his Carver High Eagles.

The Eagles didn't disappoint the enthusiastic crowd. Jimmy started the game by scoring the team's first ten points and the Eagles never looked back, winning 59-39. The starting team didn't even play in the last quarter. The Eagles had put on a "team ball" clinic. The opponents had good athletes and their players hustled, but Carver High's organized teamwork was too much. Sleepy's half-court pressure defense forced turnover after turnover which the Eagles converted into easy lay-ins. Jimmy and the rest of his teammates were doing everything right.

Kim waited for Jimmy after the game. She hugged him as he walked up to her and then she introduced him to about ten of her friends. Jimmy turned his head around to see all of his teammates smiling. His plan had worked. They were so distracted by the girls that they had forgotten about giving him a hard time.

The whole group made its way into the stands to watch the varsity game. Whereas the stands were packed for the ninth grade game, they were half empty for the varsity game. The media people were packing up their gear, and fans were shaking hands with friends as they were about to leave. The varsity players were not ignorant of this, but they understood the reason - Sleepy Phillips. Even though they understood, they still felt a bit of jealousy.

Mrs. Feen walked through the front door just as Jimmy and Jonesy were about to raid the refrigerator. "You boys only think about two things; food and basketball. Get out of that refrigerator and let me get you something to eat," she joked as she took the pots and plates from their hands. They sat at the table and told Mrs. Feen about the game as she fixed a snack for the both of them. Jimmy made his mom promise that she would try to take a day off and come to the next game. She promised that she would try. After they finished eating, all three went to bed. Mrs. Feen never mentioned anything about Jonesy sleeping at the house. She knew Ted's reputation and figured it had something to do with this.

Wednesday was another slow day for Jimmy. He thought more about the basketball team and Kim than his classes, which of course made them drag on and on. However, Jimmy was determined to win his second bet with Sleepy, so he tried to listen to the lessons and comprehend the information.

Sleepy conducted a tough practice Wednesday. He told the team they had played well the night before, but that they weren't pushed very hard. After practice Sleepy surprised Jimmy, Junior, Tommy and Jonesy by giving them the day off from their stadium duty. Sleepy didn't want to run them completely out of gas.

CHAPTER XII

Superstar In The Making

Jimmy and his mother were not able to sit and chat very often. She was either at work or running errands and he was at school, practice or running around with his friends. It was hard for her to keep up with his life. Lately though, she had noticed he had been taking books home from school and reading them before he went to bed. She was happy about this. However, she was disappointed that she hadn't been able to attend one of Jimmy's basketball games, although she had followed the season very closely through the newspapers.

Mrs. Feen was also curious about the girl Bull had mentioned the other day. She was very interested in this development in her son's life.

———————

Jimmy was thankful that Sleepy did not make them run stairs after practice. He felt like relaxing. Jimmy knew his body well and he knew it needed a rest. When he walked into his house, his mom was waiting for him in the kitchen.

"Hello, son. You're home early tonight. Anything wrong?"

"Coach Phillips let us go a little early tonight. He said we needed some rest before tomorrow night's game." Jimmy hadn't told her that he was one of four players who had to stay late because of academic difficulties. He didn't intend to tell her either.

"Good! You boys have been working hard and deserve a rest," she replied.

The two of them sat down and began to eat their dinner. Mrs. Feen didn't quite know how to approach Jimmy about this girl she had heard about, so she decided to take the direct approach.

"I heard Bull talking about some girl you have been seeing and..."

Jimmy tried to interrupt her. "Mom, Mom, let me tell you...," but Mrs. Feen wouldn't let him finish.

"Let me finish, son." Jimmy put his head down toward his plate, trying to conceal the embarrassed smile spreading across his face. Mrs. Feen continued, "I'd like to meet this girl. You invite her over here for dinner some night so we can talk." By this time she had seen the big smile on his face and she began to smile too.

"Okay, Mom, but it's no big deal. We're just friends. The guys are just giving me a hard time. You know how it is." Mrs. Feen did know how it was. She suspected her son was on the verge of having a girlfriend.

"You invite her over here tomorrow night, after the game, so I can meet her," Mrs. Feen said. Jimmy just shrugged his shoulders. "If I have to, I'll call her myself," she added. With that, both mother and son broke out in laughter. Jimmy managed to say between laughs that he would invite Kim over.

Before Jimmy went to bed, he skipped a thousand times with his jump rope and did some calf raises. The whole time he did these exercises, he thought about dunking on someone. As Jimmy was finishing, Jonesy came walking up the driveway.

"Hey, buddy, how you doing?" Jimmy greeted him.

"Not so good. Ted has got something going on again tonight," Jonesy said with a depressed look on his face. "So, I was hoping I could stay over, again."

"No problem, Jonesy, but you know you don't have to ask. That spare bedroom is yours until you don't need it anymore."

"Thanks, Jimmy, I really appreciate it." Jimmy followed in behind Jonesy and both boys got ready for bed.

Jimmy awoke early the next morning. All night, he had dreamed of the next night's game. He was rested and ready. "Too bad the game isn't in the morning," he thought to himself as he headed for the shower. When he got out of the shower, his buddies were already at the kitchen table eating breakfast. Jimmy woke Jonesy up and then headed for the kitchen table to join the crowd.

Bull had a newspaper and had started reading the sports page. "I don't believe it," was all he could say as he stared at the front page.

"What's the matter, muscle head, can't you read?" Kenny joked.

"I don't believe it," Bull said again. He turned the paper around so everyone at the table could read it. Around the table, everybody's face began to look the same as Bull's. Smack dab in the middle of the front page was a picture of Sleepy and a picture of Jimmy. The headline read, *"Basketball Great Teaches Protégé."* The article went on to recap the whole story of why Sleepy was coaching Carver High's ninth grade team. It highlighted the bet on the golf course, Sleepy's offer to coach the team, and of the team's unfolding undefeated season.

The article discussed the city's rapture over the team and also the national exposure that Sleepy Phillips was drawing. Finally, it told of Jimmy Feen and his similarities to Sleepy. The article was glowing in its respect for Sleepy and complimentary about the team's success and Jimmy's playing abilities.

Mrs. Feen wondered what all the commotion was about as she washed the dishes. She saw Jimmy and all his friends huddled around the newspaper. After they left for school, she opened the paper and smiled as a proud mother would. When she finished reading, she cut the article out and pasted it into a scrapbook she had made for Jimmy.

———————

It seemed that the whole school was talking about this night's game. Sleepy Phillips had energized George Washington Carver High School. Since Sleepy was usually only seen during the games, Jimmy began to bear the brunt of the enthusiasm. Students introduced themselves to Jimmy all day, congratulating him on the article and wishing the team good luck for the game. Teachers had special talks with him. They talked of his improved class work and, of course, basketball and Sleepy Phillips. Jimmy noticed students looking and pointing at him. Jimmy had heard people like Michael Jordan, and even Sleepy, talk about how they wished they just lived normal lives. Jimmy didn't think it was so bad. That was until he walked right into the chest of big Lucius Jackson.

Jimmy was startled as he turned a corner to see big Lucius standing right in front of him. Lucius' annoyance had been building ever since the ninth grade team, rather than the varsity, had been getting all the attention

"Hey, pretty boy. I read about you in the paper today." Jimmy could tell Lucius was mad. Lucius continued trying to intimidate Jimmy. "Let me tell you something, superstar. Bring that weak little body into the lane against me and I'll break it." Lucius then pushed Jimmy into the wall and growled.

Kim happened to walk around the corner in time to see Lucius push Jimmy. After Lucius left she came up to Jimmy.

"What was that all about?" she asked.

"I don't know, but I think I'll try to stay away from him."

"He doesn't seem to like you, but that's okay because he looked dumb anyway." Kim then leaned over on her tip toes and kissed Jimmy on the cheek.

"What was that for?" he asked, surprised that it had happened.

Kim blushed, "I don't know. I'm sorry."

"No, no, no," Jimmy said quickly. "Don't be sorry, I didn't mind."

Kim smiled shyly, relieved her gesture was welcomed. She and Jimmy then walked to their next classes which were in the same hallway.

Jimmy's teammates really let him have it at lunch time. They all bowed as he entered and chanted, "We're not worthy, we're not worthy."

Jimmy just laughed. "Ah, you guys know how it is. Just like Sleepy says, pretty soon everybody is going to forget about us."

"Don't you mean, forget about you?" Mark Abronovich asked.

Jimmy was taken back a bit by this comment. He tried his best to be a team player, but he felt he had to respond. "You guys know, just as well as I do, that Sleepy is a great coach and has helped us achieve this success. I'm just getting lucky right now. Pretty soon everybody will get their turn in the spotlight. That's what happens on a good team."

The other players on the team all respected Jimmy and appreciated that he was a team player. They also knew that he was head and shoulders above the rest of them in basketball ability.

"Don't worry about this fool," Bull said as he grabbed Mark and put him in a headlock. "I'll straighten him out. The rest of us are happy for you and are just concentrating on playing team ball and winning tonight." Jimmy knew he could count on Bull and appreciated the comments.

Jimmy's first class after lunch was Science. Mr. Barnes was teaching about electrical currents this day. As Jimmy listened to Mr. Barnes explain how a current is formed and then travels to different household appliances, he became extremely interested. He was surprised when the class bell rang. "Maybe Sleepy's right about listening in class," Jimmy thought to himself. "Time flies when you're having fun."

Before Jimmy knew it, 3:00 p.m. had rolled around and school was over. The team all met in the cafeteria for the pre-game meal and were surprised to see Sleepy waiting for them.

"Hello, men," Sleepy said. "Get something to eat and then get right back here." As the players brought their pre-game snacks back to the tables, Sleepy grabbed a stack of envelopes from his briefcase. The boys were curious as to what Sleepy was doing.

"Men, our team has been working extremely hard. I'm proud of you. So, as a reward for your hard work, I would like to invite you and your families to my house for lunch and dinner, this Saturday. In the envelopes you'll see invitations for your families. We'll all meet at the school and drive to my house together. It will be easier that way. Make sure you give these invitations to your families and then tell me how many people will be with you." Most of the players had stopped listening to Sleepy at this point. They were all dreaming about what Sleepy's house looked like. They knew he was a multimillionaire and they each had an idea about how millionaires lived.

"Hey, is anybody listening to me?" Sleepy shouted, awaking his team from their daydreams. "Now let's talk about the game tonight." As Sleepy was saying this, he heard some commotion in the back of the lunch room and turned to see the cheerleaders coming into the cafeteria. They did a quick cheer for the team and then left candy and cards for the team members. Sleepy was not amused, but he smiled at the girls anyway and waited for them to leave.

After the cheerleaders left, Sleepy got the attention of the team again and started to warn them about outside interference. "I want to tell you boys something. I don't want you worrying about girls before games because it keeps your minds off what you're supposed to be doing. Pretty soon you're going to run up against a team that wants to win more than you do and then you're going to go home sad. So no thinking about girls!" he said firmly. Sleepy realized how funny this sounded the minute he said it. Nothing in the world could make these boys not think about girls. "Let me rephrase that," he said with a chuckle. "Try not to think about them too much." The team laughed with their coach. Soon however, they were again talking basketball strategy. When they were done, Sleepy told them to meet back in the locker room in thirty minutes.

Sleepy headed for the small office in the locker room to make a few phone calls. The boys finished their snacks and continued their fantasies about Sleepy's house.

"I'll bet he has a full-court basketball floor," Mark said.

"Yeah, and it's probably indoors," Willie Stone added.

"He's got everything money can buy," Bull stated confidently. Jimmy was only half listening. He knew he should call his mom to make sure she could take off work Saturday. She wouldn't want to miss this. She always talked about buying a big house if she ever won the lottery, but Jimmy didn't put much faith in the lottery. He figured he had a better chance of working hard, signing a big NBA contract and then buying her a house. He quietly got up and made his way to the pay phone outside. As he was waiting for his mom to pick up the phone, he made up his mind to invite Kim. This was going to be a lot of fun, Jimmy figured.

Before the boys headed to the floor for their warm-ups, Sleepy reviewed what he wanted done during the game. "Defensive pressure. That's the name of this game," Sleepy said as he leaned against an old blue locker.

Sleepy wanted to pump up his team, so he continued, "You boys have a special talent. You have an ability to put extreme pressure on the other team. This is fantastic and if we can keep it up, we stand a good chance of winning the tournament and you'll have a great team all through high school. One problem I see, though, is that occasionally one person will lose his focus. What happens is that person doesn't box out or doesn't deny a passing lane and the defense breaks down. I'm hoping for a complete, one hundred-percent focus on the defensive end. Stopping the other team from getting the ball into the basket is the primary goal. If I see someone losing their focus, I'm going to replace you with someone else. This is not a threat, it's a fact. Remember, lose yourself in the game and push yourself until you sweat harder than you ever have. Then, if you need a rest, you'll have earned it."

Skits Cunningham had smelled a big story since his grandson had called and told of how Sleepy Phillips was coaching the ninth grade team. He had been trying to make contact with Sleepy ever since, but had been denied at every attempt. Skits had seen most of the games this season and had realized that there was no chance of talking to Sleepy after the game. Security was too tight. So today, he had shown up extremely early in an effort to meet with Sleepy before the game. Skits made his way to the locker room door, but just as he was about to knock, a man stepped in front of him and asked who he was.

"I'm Doc Jones, Sleepy Phillips' old high school coach. I was hoping he had a second," Skits said to the man. Skits was well beyond worrying about telling a lie. In the newspaper business, you had to do what you had to do.

"Hold on, sir, I'll relay the message," the security guard answered politely. The security guard unlocked the door, went inside and locked it behind him. Skits was impressed with the tightness of the security, but he also understood that Sleepy had to be careful because of all the crazy people in the world today.

A few minutes later the guard returned. "Mr. Phillips will be with you in a few minutes," he said. A short time later Sleepy poked his head out the door. Once he saw that it was Skits, and not his old coach, he rolled his eyes and gave a muffled laugh.

"Rudy," Sleepy said to the security guard, "you've just been fooled by a wily old sports writer. How are you doing, Skits?" Sleepy addressed Skits cordially.

"I'm doing fine. I have a grandson that goes to school here and he's a big fan of yours. He told me to get down here and cover this story."

"You can't disappoint your grandson," Sleepy quipped.

"You're right about that." Skits then got right to the point. "All the other sports writers have been writing about you, but I want to write about the interplay between you and the kids. How everybody gets along. How you coach them. The real inside scoop." Skits was confused by Sleepy's blank expression. "Well, what do you say?" Skits asked.

Sleepy looked up at the ceiling and started laughing. He stepped back into the locker room and addressed the team. "Boys, we have a sports reporter here named Skits Cunningham. Skits has been writing for the *St. Louis Times* for thirty years." As Sleepy was talking, Skits had made his way into the center of the locker room.

"Thirty-three years," Skits corrected him.

Sleepy nodded. "Anyways, he wants to do an inside story on our team. I figured I would let you guys decide for yourselves if you wanted a reporter hanging around."

"I think it would be great," Kenny blurted out. "If you want a real good interview, my name is...," but Bull put his hand over Kenny's mouth so he couldn't finish. Everybody, including Sleepy and Skits, laughed.

"Well, what do you guys think?" Sleepy asked.

"It would be cool," Bull said.

"Yeah, but are you going to interview everybody or just Sleepy?" Too Tall asked skeptically.

"Good question," Skits answered. "I want to interview everyone and get to know the team. I want to know what this team is really about, the coach and the players."

The boys were nodding their heads with approval. "Okay Skits, I guess you can do it," Sleepy said. "However, I've been warning these boys about you media people, so you better not try to pull anything funny." Skits looked hurt by this comment, but Sleepy didn't care. He had been burned so many times by self-serving sports writers that he had learned to be on guard. "Skits, if you call me tomorrow at the school, we'll set up the logistics of this whole thing," Sleepy said to Skits as he ushered him out the locker room door. Skits thanked everyone and as he walked out, he felt like he had just landed a great article.

After Skits left, Sleepy sent his team to the court. As he passed the security guard, Sleepy stopped. "I don't care if someone says they're my grandmother, don't let them in," he said with a growl. The security guard nodded sheepishly.

As usual, the opposing coach came over to Sleepy before the game and asked for his autograph. Meanwhile, the players on the opposing team stared at him. Sleepy was used to this by now. It happened every game. After this period of awkwardness, the boys on the other team began their usual pre-game drills.

Sleepy walked underneath the Eagles' basket and watched his team do lay-ups. While standing there he looked around the gymnasium. Banners were hanging everywhere. "Sleepy's Flying Eagles," one read. Another said, "Jimmy Feen, the next Sleepy Phillips." The cheerleaders were doing cheers and the band was playing. Television crews were courtside doing their stories and, as usual, Sleepy's bodyguards were seated all along the front row in case anybody was thinking of being crazy. This was definitely the place to be in St. Louis. It was an event.

Skits Cunningham knew the reason for this happening. Skits knew that Sleepy was so famous he could attract this kind of attention. However, Skits had been around this business a long time and he also knew the importance of winning. Because these young kids were undefeated and playing very exciting basketball, they added to the attraction. Skits felt this was where the big story was waiting. Not in Sleepy himself, but in the team.

The horn sounded and the players ran back to their benches. Sleepy had been watching the other team do warm-ups. They looked small, but quick. He passed this observation along to his players. Sleepy mentioned that against a smaller team, working the ball inside was the correct strategy. "Cutters go hard toward the front of the rim. Too Tall, look for backdoor cuts if the defense plays tight on Jimmy and Kenny," Sleepy instructed. Too Tall nodded his head, signaling he understood Sleepy's last-minute instructions. The teams headed for center court and the opening tip.

The first quarter went exactly as Sleepy had thought. The opposing team used quickness and speed to disrupt Kenny's and Jonesy's ball handling. When the Eagles did successfully work the ball up the court, Too Tall and Bull simply overpowered their defensive men for easy lay-ins. At the end of the first quarter, the score was tied 15-15.

Sleepy directed his team to be more careful with the ball, but the second quarter was more of the same. Sleepy sensed that Kenny was getting tired trying to dribble the ball up the court against the tough defense. He called for Tommy Peterson to get into the game and replace Kenny. Tommy had good speed and quickness, but the opposing coach sensed Tommy's inexperience and applied a full-court press.

Jimmy was not tired, but he was becoming frustrated. Every time he touched the ball, two opposing players would guard him, forcing him to pass to someone else. The other team's strategy was obviously to limit Jimmy's possessions. The opposing team, on the strength of their full-court press, took a 39-29 lead into the halftime break. Bull led the Eagles with nine points.

Sleepy knew this was his team's first real test since their opening game. His boys would give one hundred percent effort, but they needed more than that. They needed to break the full-court press with crisp passing and hard drives to the basket.

"Sit down, men," he said as he rolled the blackboard out from behind one of the lockers. "How does it feel to be outplayed for the first half?" he asked them seriously. Sleepy could tell by looking at their faces that his team was disheartened. Sleepy was not discouraged however, but he did want his team to understand they were outplayed because of lack of execution. "Don't worry, gentlemen," Sleepy reassured them. "It's the first time it has happened all year. Now I want to make something very clear. They didn't out hustle you, they just played better." The boys didn't quite understand what Sleepy was getting at, but they could feel his energy building. The locker room was deadly silent except for Sleepy's voice.

Sleepy continued talking as he drew an outline of the entire court on the blackboard. "No problem, that's why we play two halves, but if we don't get smart, we're going to lose this game, so listen up." Sleepy began explaining how to successfully break a full-court press. He drew players on the blackboard and showed them where to move and how to get the ball to another player.

"Quick passes. Quick passes," he kept repeating. Sleepy instructed the ball to be passed to Kenny about six feet from the sideline. "Any closer and you'll get trapped," Sleepy said. Sleepy then detailed how Jonesy was to fake a cut to the middle of the floor and then head straight for Kenny on the same sideline. "Kenny, you should pass the ball to Jonesy as soon as you see him break towards you. The sooner you get him the ball, the better."

Sleepy motioned for Bull to stand up. "Bull, you're going to hurry to the three-point line after you inbound the ball. As soon as you see Kenny pass the ball to Jonesy, you need to sprint down the center of the floor and look for a pass from

Jonesy. Once you get the ball, you, Too Tall and Jimmy should have a two-on-three fast break."

Sleepy was becoming animated now. He was moving all around the room, imitating the movements he was telling his team to make. He was excited and his team was feeding on that energy. "All we have to do is get the ball to the middle of the court with our momentum going towards the basket. Once we have that, then the other team is in a defensive posture. We have to keep them guessing and we have to go hard to the hole."

Sleepy turned his back to the team, took a few deep breaths and then turned to face them again. He was psyching himself up. "If you really want to win this game, I'll tell you how." The boys shouted their approval.

"Good. Now the way to win is to get the ball to the middle of the floor like I just described. However, more important than that is to get dirty on defense. We have a great defensive team that can shut people down, but we lost our focus on doing that in the first half. We were more concerned with their defensive pressure. Get in their faces. Give them some of their own medicine, but give it to them harder. Commit to be in their faces every time they get the ball. Predict how they're going to dribble and take the ball away. Take the ball away by getting in their faces and playing tougher defense than they have ever seen." Sleepy was shouting at the end of this speech and his players were itching to get on the floor. He had fired them up and now they were ready to do battle.

Jimmy looked into the stands as he walked out onto the floor for the second half. He saw all the people rooting for him. He saw Kim clapping and smiling at him from the top

row of the bleachers. He smiled back. Jimmy then put his
head down and lost himself in the game.

The opposing team got the ball first. They worked the ball
around the court until one of their guards made a fifteen-foot
jump shot. The opposing team then went straight back to their
pressing style defense.

Bull in-bounded the ball to Kenny, who was breaking for
the sideline. Kenny faked a pass back to Bull and then bounced
a perfect pass to Jonesy, who was coming straight towards
him on the sideline. Jonesy pivoted with the ball and then
spotted Bull sprinting up the center of the court, his defensive
player two steps behind. Jonesy flipped the ball to Bull. They
had broken the press beautifully and now it was a three-on-
two with Jimmy gliding toward the basket on one side and Too
Tall lumbering down the other.

Bull rushed towards the foul line and then stopped. The
defenders were caught in the middle of their reactions and this
enabled Bull to toss the ball to Jimmy. Jimmy dribbled once
and then leaped into the air, rising past the last defender. As
he soared towards the rim, the gymnasium became quiet. All
eyes were on him. Jimmy gripped the ball in his right hand
and as he elevated higher than the basket, he cocked his arm
back and then whipped down a vicious dunk. The crowd
exploded in a thunderous cheer. Little kids watching the game
stood up and gave each other high fives. It was a big-time play.

Jimmy's slam dunk started one of the greatest halves in St.
Louis high school basketball history. The play ignited the team
and Jimmy. The Eagles continued to get the ball past the press
and Jimmy used all of his moves to dumbfound the opponents.
He scored a record twenty points in the third quarter alone,

with three baskets coming on dunks. He added ten more points in the fourth quarter as the Eagles built a sixteen-point lead. Sleepy pulled Jimmy from the game with just over three minutes remaining. As he walked off the floor, the crowd rose and gave him a standing ovation. Sleepy stopped him before he sat down.

"How does it feel?" he asked Jimmy.

"Good," Jimmy replied. Sleepy knew that Jimmy had lost himself in the game.

"Good game, Jimmy," Sleepy said as he patted his star player on the back.

When Jimmy came out of the locker room after the game, Kim and her parents were waiting for him.

"Hello, Jimmy, I'm Kim's dad," Mr. Williams said, introducing himself.

"Hello, sir," Jimmy replied as he shook his hand.

"Kim told me you were a good basketball player, but I didn't think you would be that good. Great game," Mr. Williams said. Kim's mom then kissed Jimmy on both sides of the face. This caught Jimmy by surprise.

"My mom is from Brazil," Kim laughed. "It's a custom to kiss people on both cheeks when you see them."

"Okay," Jimmy said, still looking a bit surprised.

"My mom and dad are going to drop us off at your house tonight after the varsity game. They also want to invite your mom and dad to our house tomorrow for dinner." Jimmy realized that Kim didn't yet know about his father.

"Thanks," he replied simply.

The varsity team won their game by the score of 82-71. After the game, Kim's mother and father took Jimmy home. During the ride they talked mostly about basketball and Sleepy Phillips. Jimmy wasn't surprised. Everybody he talked to wanted to know about Sleepy.

Jimmy walked to the front door and held it open for Kim and her parents. Mrs. Feen was standing in the kitchen, cooking dinner. Jimmy hoped his mom wouldn't be mad at him. She wasn't expecting Kim's parents.

"Hi, Mom," Jimmy said as Mrs. Feen turned around. "This is Kim Williams and her parents. They gave me a ride home from the game," Jimmy said, trying to offer an explanation of why they were here unexpectedly.

"Hello, Kim. I've been hearing a lot about you lately," Mrs. Feen said warmly. "How are you folks doing?" Mrs. Feen then asked Kim's parents.

"Very good, thank you," Mrs. Williams replied.

"How was the game?" Mrs. Feen asked her son. Before Jimmy could answer, Mr. Williams answered for him.

"Your son was the star of the game. He played the best game I've ever seen from a high school player."

Mrs. Feen smiled widely when she heard this. "Can you stay for dinner?" she asked Kim's parents.

"No, we really can't, but thank you very much," Mrs. Williams answered quickly. "We only stopped to drop Jimmy and Kim off and to invite you over for dinner tomorrow night."

"Well, thank you very much. I might have to work, but I'll let Jimmy know in time to tell Kim tomorrow," Mrs. Feen replied gracefully. Mr. and Mrs. Williams said goodbye and left, leaving Kim at the Feen's house.

Kim, Mrs. Feen and Jimmy sat down at the table for dinner. Mrs. Feen tried to get Jimmy to tell her about the game, but he only told her general details. Jimmy wasn't one to talk about himself, but Kim told Mrs. Feen everything.

Mrs. Feen liked Kim, and her parents seemed nice, too, but she told Kim that she wouldn't be able to attend dinner the next night. Mrs. Feen did not like to miss work, and she had already switched with someone else so she could go with Jimmy to Sleepy's house Saturday. Jimmy asked Kim if she wanted to go too. She quickly accepted. After dinner, Kim and Mrs. Feen sat on the couch and talked while Jimmy mostly listened. Later in the evening, Mrs. Feen and Jimmy drove Kim home.

CHAPTER XIII

Living Large

Bull liked to sneak into Jimmy's room while Jimmy was still asleep and play pranks on him. Bull had been playing these tricks for over ten years, but Jimmy never got mad. This morning, however, Jimmy was lying awake in bed, faking sleep. He saw Bull slowly open the door and creep in. Just as Bull was about to pour water on him, Jimmy reached out and grabbed Bull. Bull jumped back, spilling the water all over himself.

"I didn't know you were awake."

"Obviously," Jimmy laughed as he made his way out of bed and into the shower. Jimmy saw Bull open the guest door in order to awaken Jonesy. By the time Jimmy made it to the kitchen, Tommy Peterson and Junior Hernandez had already taken their seats.

"Hey, it's the superstar," Junior joked. Bull held up the sports page for Jimmy to read. It had a picture of Jimmy dunking. *"Fifteen Year-Old Phenom Leads Sleepy's Team To Victory,"* the headline read.

"We better not get caught up in what the papers are saying or somebody is going to whip our butts in the tournament," Jimmy said while barely looking at the paper. The friends agreed and as Mrs. Feen put the food on the table, the talking stopped and the eating started. During periods when the boys didn't have too much food in their mouths, they discussed the trip to Sleepy's house. They were all very excited about it.

———————————

Sleepy worked the boys hard in practice this day. He had them do a variety of exhausting running drills until each player was ready to drop. Sleepy showed some compassion by letting Jimmy, Tommy, Kenny and Jonesy have the night off from running the stairs again.

"He's trying to kill us," Kenny said as he started his usual bellyaching on the walk home.

"Quit crying," Bull said. "Coach is just trying to get us ready for the tournament."

"Bull's right," Jimmy chipped in. "Sleepy wants us to be in peak condition so we can play our best."

"He wants us to be able to lose ourselves in the game," Tommy said, imitating Sleepy's voice. This drew a laugh from everybody.

"Jimmy, do you mind if I stay over again tonight?" Jonesy asked as the group entered their neighborhood. "You know I can't get any sleep with Ted acting crazy, and I don't want to fall asleep at Sleepy's tomorrow."

"No problem. Just knock on the door and tell my Mom you're going to stay. I'm going to Kim's house for dinner tonight so I won't be there until later. But what do you say when I get back, we all go to the courts for some game.

"Sounds good to me," Bull said.

"Yeah, we'll go too," Tommy and Junior joined in.

"How about I meet you at the courts and then go to your house afterwards," Jonesy suggested.

"Good idea," Jimmy responded.

One by one, the boys headed up their driveways. Bull waited until only he and Jimmy were left. "You're getting pretty serious with this girl," Bull stated to Jimmy.

"We're just friends," Jimmy said unconvincingly.

"No problem, buddy," Bull laughed, "just don't let her keep you away from the courts. The reason you're getting all this attention is because of all those late nights we practiced. Don't forget," he warned.

Jimmy laughed. "Don't worry about me. Worry about yourself when I dunk on you tonight."

"You must be daydreaming again," Bull kidded as he and Jimmy headed up their respective driveways.

Jimmy's mom took him over to Kim's around 7:30 p.m. Jimmy met Kim's little brother and looked at old photo albums of Kim. Jimmy also found out that Kim's dad was a lawyer downtown, although, he was much more interested in what was going on at Sleepy Phillips' house the next afternoon than any court case he was working on.

"So what does Sleepy have planned for tomorrow?" he asked Jimmy.

"Nobody really knows anything. Sleepy just said he was having a party and serving food," Jimmy answered.

Mr. Williams was a big fan of Sleepy's and joked that he wished he could go. "Don't worry, Dad. I'll tell you all about it," Kim assured her father. Jimmy had a great time, but by 9:30 p.m. he was ready to go.

As Mr. Williams approached Jimmy's home, Jimmy told him to go straight and drop him off at the basketball courts.

"Are you going to be all right?" Kim's dad asked. He knew it was a tough neighborhood.

"Don't worry, Mr. Williams, this is where I live. I play here every night."

"Okay Jimmy," Kim's dad replied with a hint of embarrassment. Kim surprised Jimmy again by kissing him on the cheek as he got out of the car.

Bull, Jonesy, Junior, Kenny and Tommy were already at the courts. They all saw Kim kiss Jimmy as he got out of the car, and when he came walking down to the courts they started giving him a hard time. Usually, Jimmy was the first one to the courts, but tonight he was last and the guys let him have it.

When the older guys heard the chatter and learned it was aimed towards Jimmy Feen, they started in on him too. Pretty soon, everybody at the courts was messing with Jimmy. Most of it was in good humor, although a couple of the varsity players were there and their kidding had a hard edge to it.

"You all can mess with me if you want, but I'm here to play some ball," Jimmy said with a smirk as he picked up a loose ball and went to an open court. The usual Friday night routine was in effect. Winners stayed on the court and the losers sat down.

Kim's parents drove into the Feen's driveway at 8:00 a.m. the next morning. They walked Kim to the door and were surprised to see about fifteen people in the house laughing and listening to music. The whole neighborhood gang and their parents had decided to meet at the Feen's house before they left for Sleepy's. It looked like a party and Jimmy's mom was right in the middle of it. She was grabbing empty plates from Jimmy and all his friends. She saw Kim and her parents at the door and waved them in.

"Boy, you sure do entertain a big crowd," Mrs. Williams said as she greeted Jimmy's mom.

"Oh yes," Mrs. Feen replied, "but it's been like this for years. Everybody here is like family to Jimmy and me." Jimmy introduced Kim's parents to everyone and then the whole group started filing into cars, ready to head for the school to meet Sleepy.

When Jimmy and his group pulled into the high school parking lot, all the other team members and their guests were already there. Sleepy was standing off to the side of two large buses, trying to get people to take seats on them. However, most of the player's guests had never met Sleepy, so many of them were standing around staring at him or asking for autographs.

"Can I have your attention, everyone?" Sleepy shouted loudly. His players all knew he was getting a bit frustrated because that was the type of voice he used in practice sometimes. "Please get onto the buses. We are going to spend most of the day together, so if you want an autograph, get it later," he said bluntly. "We have to get going, so please, get on a bus." Everyone then began taking their seats.

Sleepy explained that the party would end around 8:00 p.m. and that the buses would take them back to the school parking lot. "Sit back and relax," he added, "the ride will take about forty-five minutes."

The buses weaved their way in and out of traffic until, finally, they began to leave the city and head into the outlying rural area of St. Louis. Jimmy had his nose smashed up against the window as he looked at all of the open land. He didn't see this area all that often. Most of the time he was within the city limits.

Kim was looking out the window too, but not as intently as Jimmy. "What are you thinking about?" she finally asked him.

"I'm going to live on land like this someday, just peace and quiet," he answered her.

The buses turned onto a road lined with oak trees on both sides. As they headed up the road, they began to leave all the houses behind and soon came upon a big lake surrounded by woods. It was a magnificent sight. The large oak trees with their long, curling branches lined the road leading to the lake. The lake itself was so still it seemed to have been painted.

Everyone was so taken by the beauty of these surroundings that they were surprised when the buses stopped in front of two, extremely large and lavishly decorated iron gates. The gates opened automatically as two guards waved to Sleepy. The gates closed behind them. A large brick wall extended out from both sides of the iron gates, encompassing the entire estate. Once the buses had traveled over a small hill, Sleepy and his guests could see his home.

The house looked like an English mansion. Built with red brick, all three stories were partly covered with moss. A guest house, the size of most regular homes, was set off about twenty-five yards to the side. Large oak trees covered the entire front lawn. Off in the distance, near the lake, six horses were being led out of the covered stables. Sleepy's house was the only one in sight. It was a beautiful home.

Sleepy sprang out of the bus and told everyone to gather around. He was about to address the group when he heard a sound behind him. It was his wife and two daughters.

"Everyone, I would like to introduce you to my wife, Sandra, and my two daughters, Elexis and Alexandra. Elexis looked to be around eighteen years old and Alexandra, fourteen. Mrs. Phillips went over and held her husband's hand and addressed the group.

"I want to thank you all for coming. Sleepy has been talking so much about these boys, we just figured it was time to have some sort of party and this seemed like the right way to do it. Please everybody, make yourselves at home. You can go anywhere you like, the stables, the recording room, anywhere. If you have any questions, just ask. Now, first of all, we have a brunch ready, so if anybody is hungry, follow me."

Mrs. Feen could tell she liked Sandra Phillips already. She was obviously a rich woman, but she seemed down-to-Earth and had a real nice way about her. Mrs. Feen also noticed that her daughters were pretty, just like their mother.

Bull nudged Jimmy. "This place is awesome. Sleepy definitely has got some taste." The entire busload of people were in awe of Sleepy's home. They knew that Sleepy was a multimillionaire, but they had no idea that he lived this extravagantly.

Mrs. Phillips had organized a huge brunch on the enclosed back patio. Long sets of tables and chairs were covered with large trays containing scrambled eggs, bacon, pancakes, sausages, potatoes, breads and cereal. Every kind of food one could imagine eating for lunch or breakfast was spread out before them. A team of caterers had been hired to prepare and serve the food. They were kept busy refilling orange juice glasses, retrieving silverware and generally putting up with a bunch of fifteen year-olds and their parents.

"What do you think, Mom? Could you live like this?" Jimmy asked his mother who was sitting across from him.

"I don't know, but I'd sure like to try it for a while," she answered wishfully.

It was a beautiful morning and everyone enjoyed the meal. After brunch, Sleepy invited all his guests to wander about. "As my wife said when you first got here, make yourselves at home. Play in the game room. Ride the horses. Have a good time. We'll be eating again around four-thirty, so meet back here." Sleepy looked content as his guests began to wander in all directions.

"Wow," Kenny said in awe as he stood in front of the biggest television he had ever seen. Surrounding the television was a large set of speakers. The speakers, together with the television, filled the whole wall. Kenny spotted a Nintendo GameCube® on one of the shelves and grabbed it. Tommy turned it on and put a basketball game in. They began to play. The players on the screen were at least six feet tall and compared to Kenny and Tommy, who were sitting down, it looked like something out of a futuristic movie.

Jimmy, Mrs. Feen and Kim made their way around the entire house. Mrs. Feen was speechless. It was a beautiful home, the kind she had dreamed about her entire life. Jimmy wished he could buy her one. One day, he told himself, he would.

Kim especially liked the music room. There were compact discs everywhere. CD holders had been built right into the walls and they surrounded the entire room. Video screens were placed throughout the room and a dance floor was hidden in the corner, with the full assortment of strobe lights and smoke machines. Kim knew that Sandra Phillips had thrown some cool parties down here.

Sleepy's guests were impressed by the magnificent home, but it was the building that acted as the stable and the boathouse that had them gawking. Horses on one side and two large boats on the other. The boats were actually floating inside the building, and large doors led to the open waters. Around 4:00 p.m., everyone headed to the patio for dinner. Sleepy, Sandra and their two girls were seated at one of the many tables, waiting for everyone to show up.

"I hope everyone has had a good time," Sleepy said as he stood up and addressed all sixty of the people who had come. "To tell you the truth, it has been my pleasure. The kids that play on the team have been a real inspiration for me and I wanted to thank them." Sleepy looked down at his wife because he knew he was getting emotional. She was looking up at him with total love and commitment.

Mrs. Feen never noticed Sleepy getting emotional or heard any of his words. She wanted to know where Jimmy was. He was right behind her as they walked up the yard to be seated for dinner. Mrs. Feen looked at Kim. Their eyes met and both knew that the other was thinking the same thing. Where was Jimmy?

After Sleepy finished his speech, the caterers served the food. "Where do you think he went?" Mrs. Feen asked Kim.

Kim didn't know. Mrs. Feen got up from her chair and walked over to Sleepy's table. "Excuse me," she said.

Sleepy and Sandra both jumped up. "Yes Mrs. Feen," Sandra answered. "Is everything okay?"

"Well, it seems I don't know where Jimmy is," Mrs. Feen replied. Sleepy was puzzled.

"I know it sounds strange, but this is a big house and maybe he got lost or something," Mrs. Feen stated.

Sleepy and Sandra and their two daughters split up and went looking around the house. Sleepy wondered what this was all about. Jimmy wasn't one to make a scene. Sleepy held Jimmy in high regards. He was a hard worker, a fair young man and seemed to be a good son. "Where in the world is he?" Sleepy said out loud.

Sandra checked the kitchen, the pool house, the arcade and the tennis courts. Her two daughters checked the bedrooms, the living room, the family room, and the rest of the living quarters. Sleepy first looked in the recording studio, but then thought a moment more. Sleepy knew exactly where Jimmy was. Sleepy headed for the basement. He knew no one had checked there.

Jimmy couldn't believe his eyes. Sleepy definitely had a nice house and a lot of money, but this was too cool. Jimmy was standing in the middle of Sleepy's full-court basketball floor. Glass backboards and hardwood floors. There were over one hundred spacious leather spectator seats. Jimmy moved to the three-point line and picked up a stray ball.

"Don't shoot unless you're going to make it," Sleepy called to Jimmy.

Jimmy turned quickly, surprised by the voice. When he saw it was Sleepy, he turned back around and swished the shot.

———————————————

As Sleepy waved goodbye to all of the families, he felt a real bond with his team. For their part, the player's parents felt as if their boys were playing for someone who really cared about them.

CHAPTER XIV

The Tournament

Sleepy started Monday's practice with some slow stretching to get his players loose. After stretching out, they walked through their man-to-man trap defense and their triangle plays on offense. The rest of practice consisted mostly of low-post defensive drills and denying-the-passing lane drills. Sleepy pushed the kids very hard. His plan was to push them hard Monday, Tuesday, and Wednesday and then go easy on them Thursday and Friday, allowing them to rest a little before their first tournament game Saturday morning.

The team was very excited. To go along with the two week Christmas vacation, the team had a week-long tournament to play in. No school and plenty of basketball. It couldn't have been any better for Jimmy and his teammates. A five-day tournament for ninth grade teams was not only unusual, but unheard of. Everyone involved knew that Sleepy was paying all of the bills, but Sleepy wasn't commenting. Whatever the reason for the tournament, the Eagles and the rest of the ninth grade teams in the state were looking forward to it.

Before the teachers had left for their vacations, Sleepy checked on the academic progress of his players. Tommy's teachers told Sleepy that Tommy was doing better, but he still needed work. Sleepy could have guessed that, but he was happy progress was being made.

Jimmy's teachers were impressed by his turnaround. "There are worse things than playing some hoop in the neighborhood," Sleepy thought to himself as he assumed he would lose another bet to Jimmy.

Jonesy had also improved in his teachers' eyes. It looked like he was getting more sleep and Sleepy was glad to hear that he wasn't messing around with drugs. All in all, it was a good week for Sleepy. The only dark spot was Skits Cunningham.

Sleepy didn't really want Skits hanging around the team during the tournament, but the kids did, so Sleepy let them have their way. It wasn't that Sleepy didn't like Skits, because he did. However, Skits was relentless when going after a story, sometimes relentless to the point of being rude. Sleepy just hoped Skits would write a nice article about the boys on the team and how they did in the tournament. Sleepy meant to keep an eye on Skits and if he sensed that Skits was adversely affecting the team, he was going to throw him out.

Jimmy was also having a good week, for the most part. He and Kim continued to see each other. Jimmy had never had a steady girlfriend, so the whole situation was a bit strange for him. They had a great time together and Jimmy really enjoyed her company, so he figured everything was cool. Kim was thinking the same way.

Jimmy did have a problem on his mind though. He was worried about Jonesy and his situation at home. Everybody on the street knew his brother, Ted, was selling drugs. Jonesy was staying at Jimmy's house every night now. Jimmy didn't mind, and neither did Mrs. Feen, but the influence Ted had on Jonesy wasn't good. Something had to be done before Ted ended up in jail, or even worse, dead.

Sleepy had a surprise for his team. They already knew about the tournament, but they didn't know that he had rented out an entire floor of a downtown hotel for the kids to stay in. Sleepy knew he had gone a little overboard, but if these kids would learn to focus on important endeavors, they could win this tournament as well as succeed in life. Sleepy liked all of these young men, so he had no trouble spending the money on the hotel. There were even rumors that Sleepy was paying the travel expenses for all the teams.

The kids met Sleepy Saturday morning at 6:00 a.m. in the school parking lot. They were scheduled to play at 10:00 a.m. Sleepy figured a light breakfast at the hotel would start the day off right. Bull, Jimmy, Jonesy, Kenny, Junior and Tommy were the first players at school.

"You boys are here early," Sleepy said. "You must be ready for the game today."

"Yes sir, we are," they all replied. As they put their bags into the bus, the other players began to arrive. Shortly thereafter the bus pulled out for the thirty-minute drive.

The players were under the impression that the team would commute to the games each day. About halfway into the drive, Sleepy stood up and addressed the team. "I got word that the seedings came out last night. We are ranked number two," he said dryly. The players erupted, voicing their displeasure. The kids were badmouthing the referees, the other teams, anybody they could think of. "Settle down, settle down," Sleepy said after letting them rant and rave for about five minutes. Sleepy noted the reaction of his team. They were not happy about this. He decided to use this as a motivator throughout the tournament. After the boys had settled down, Sleepy continued. "This is a single-elimination tournament. If we lose, we go home, so there will be no half-stepping. I have no doubt that if we play together, as a team, we can win this thing and stay here all seven days. However, you have to lose yourselves in the game." Sleepy smiled as he said this because he knew the boys had made a running joke about the saying.

The boys did chuckle, but they were intent on what Sleepy was saying. They were quiet so he continued. "I have so much faith in this team that I have rented a whole floor at the best hotel in town for seven days and nights. We'll stay there and won't leave until we've won the tournament," Sleepy said with a strong, confident voice. This confidence spread to the team. It was all Sleepy could do to calm them down as the bus pulled into the hotel's entrance.

The entire team began to stare outside at the beautiful five-star hotel. Each player had brought only one bag since they hadn't known they were going to stay in a hotel. Sleepy had told their parents of his plans at the house party and they agreed to bring extra clothes for the boys. Mrs. Feen would bring Jonesy's. As the boys jumped off the bus, doormen quickly took their bags and carried them to the front desk.

The hotel staff knew Sleepy and his team of ninth graders were coming. They had read all about the team in the newspapers and were extremely friendly to the boys. As usual,

Sleepy was hounded until he signed autographs and shook hands with almost everyone.

The manager came and introduced himself to Sleepy and then led the entire team through the lobby to the breakfast room. In front of the boys stood a huge table with fruits, juices, cereals and breads. Sleepy had specially requested light foods so the boys would not over eat and have slow reactions for the game.

After everybody had finished breakfast, Sleepy had them gather in a small lounge, off to the side of the lobby. There he gave the boys their room assignments. Jimmy and Jonesy were to stay together in room 203. Sleepy also set the rules for their stay. "There will be absolutely no leaving the premises of this building unless everybody goes or I give you special permission," he warned them. "I will not tolerate immature behavior that disturbs other guests, such as running in the hallways, food fights, or midnight kitchen raids. You will act like mature adults." Sleepy was very serious as he spoke in a stern voice. "If anybody breaks these rules he's going home and will not play in the tournament. No question about it." The boys were quiet. Sleepy had gotten their attention with his strict rules.

Sleepy looked around at his team, satisfied that he had made his point. "Now that I have scared you, let me say I don't expect any trouble. You boys are good boys and I trust you. Now remember, we have a game in approximately two hours, so go up and settle into your rooms and be back here in 30 minutes." Sleepy handed the room keys out one by one. After getting himself situated in his room, Sleepy headed back down to the lounge. He bought a newspaper and began reading the front page, only to be interrupted.

"Sleepy Phillips, how are you doing today? Is the team ready to win it all?" Skits Cunningham asked as he dragged his suitcase towards Sleepy.

"You're here early," Sleepy teased him. "I didn't know sports writers had alarm clocks." Sleepy knew that Skits would be coming to the hotel. Sleepy had acquiesced and allowed Skits to stay with the team, although Skits had to pay his own way.

"I had to get up early," Skits replied. "I'm getting the story everybody else wants. Can't miss out on that."

"I guess not," Sleepy said while rolling his eyes, not yet fully convinced that Skits was going to get this "big story."

The team arrived at the gym a little past 9:00 a.m. Most of the boys had never been to the Arena so they were antsy to get a look at it. They entered the front door and the security guards let them pass straight through when they recognized Sleepy. As soon as they entered through the doors, the boys could hear the sound of basketball being played. The squeaking shoes, the sound of a ball hitting a hardwood floor and cheering fans. The entire team walked straight towards the railing and looked down below. Jimmy couldn't believe how close the players looked. The floor was brightly lit and the colors of the uniforms, the banners, and the surrounding bleachers made the whole scene seem like a movie.

Each of the boys was thinking how big the Arena looked. Sleepy was thinking just the opposite. The Arena seated only 8,000 people. Sleepy had played in arenas three times as large for the last fifteen years of his life.

"Don't be scared, fellas," Sleepy said as he realized his boys were a little intimidated by the surroundings. "Once you start playing and begin concentrating on the opponent, you'll forget about where you are playing. I'll bet you can jump higher on this floor too," he added. Sleepy knew boys this age were always worried about how high they could jump. Sleepy wasn't lying either. He always felt like he jumped better in an arena versus a small gym.

Sleepy led the team downstairs to the locker room. Skits was following along, observing everything. Again, the boys were awed by the size of the locker room. They looked at the whirlpool equipment and the weight room. They were greatly impressed. Sleepy herded them into the changing area and had them get ready.

"Man, this place is fantastic," Kenny said excitedly.

"Yeah," Too Tall said. "I don't even have to duck under the doorways."

Jimmy laughed. "That's a good thing, Too Tall, but coach is right. We have to play just like we do on our own court. We have to lose ourselves in what we are doing. Just because the gym is bigger doesn't make any difference. The rules are the same. We're in great shape and we play as a team." Everyone was listening intently. Jimmy didn't speak much, but when he did, people listened. Jimmy was getting himself psyched up and it was carrying over to his teammates.

"I want to win this tournament," Jimmy said emphatically. "I think we can be a great team throughout high school and it all starts right here. Are we going to fold in the big games or rise to the occasion? I'm going to rise. Let's come out right from the start and give it everything we have. Let's show all these other teams what playing basketball is all about. Let's play hard. Let's be hard."

Willie Stone stood up and yelled. He didn't yell any particular word, he just roared like a lion. Mark Abronovich started too. Pretty soon the whole team was just making noise. Sleepy had walked back into the locker room to tell his team to hit the floor just as the players began to make all of the noise. He sneaked a peek around the corner and saw them giving each other high fives. Sleepy figured he would skip the pep talk. They were ready.

Sleepy turned the corner and walked into the middle of the group. The boys became silent. Sleepy just looked at them and smiled. "Hit the floor," he said as he tossed Jimmy the ball.

If anything, the excitement over Sleepy coaching a ninth grade basketball team had grown over the course of the season. The undefeated record and the emergence of Jimmy as a high school phenom caught and held the attention of the whole city. As with the regular season games, the opposing coach, the referees and whoever else happened to be on the floor all wanted to meet Sleepy as he emerged from the locker room.

After chatting with the opposing coach at center court, Sleepy walked towards the bench. As he came nearer to the bench, the flashbulbs of what seemed to be hundreds of cameras blinded Sleepy for a few moments. Sleepy was still having trouble believing that people were this interested in a ninth grade team.

Sleepy turned his attention to the opposing team. They looked big and tall. "We should be able to trap these guys," Sleepy reasoned. Sleepy knew the key to beating teams with big and strong players was to run them until they were tired.

After they were tired, they were not nearly as strong. The buzzer sounded and the team huddled around Sleepy.

"All right, fellas," Sleepy said. "You guys wanted to be the number-one seed, so go out and show everybody that you should have been. Lose yourself in what you're doing out there, whether it be playing defense or setting picks. Do whatever it takes to make the play successful. Fight for loose balls. Sprint for the other end of the court." Kenny and Tommy were giving each other high fives and slapping Jimmy on the back. Sleepy sensed his boys were ready.

"One last thing," Sleepy said as the referee waved the players to the court, "these guys are big, so run them down. Trap them all over the floor and get those loose balls." The players on both teams met at half court and shook hands with one another. The referee threw the ball up at center court to start the game and the opposing team's center controlled the tip. The opposition passed the ball straight inside to their center in the low post. Too Tall was actually a bit shorter than the other player. It was the first time this had happened all year. The opposing center faked to his left, took a long step back and banked a short jump shot into the basket for the first two points of the game.

The Eagles pushed the ball back up to their end of the court. Kenny tried to force a pass inside to Bull, but the ball was deflected out of bounds by the defender.

Jimmy sensed that the person guarding him was a little excited. The guy was trash talking a little bit and was nose to nose with Jimmy. Jimmy didn't get mad, but he did mean to slow the guy down. Jimmy remembered what Sleepy had taught them throughout the year. If your man was excited, you could beat him backdoor. As the Eagles set up for their out-of-bounds play, Sleepy called out for play number two. Kenny made sure everyone heard the call. Jimmy threw the ball in to Kenny, who had broken open at the top of the key. Jimmy wandered toward the sideline. He looked lazily up into the stands. This was all part of the play.

Jimmy stood there seemingly out of the play. His defensive man relaxed a little also. Suddenly, as if shot out of a cannon, Jimmy raced toward the foul line. Kenny saw him and began to pass the ball. The defensive player guarding Jimmy was caught flat-footed and had to race to catch up with Jimmy. Just as the defensive man came within arms reach of him, Jimmy planted his foot and broke back towards the basket. Kenny gave Jimmy a good, solid chest pass. Jimmy took the pass in stride and with one tremendous leap, reached high in the air and stuffed it through the basket. The crowd erupted. The defensive player guarding Jimmy was left standing at the foul line.

Skits Cunningham was amazed. He had watched many of the Eagles' games this year, but Jimmy Feen kept surprising him. Skits knew talent when he saw it and this kid was something special. The Eagles jumped all over the other team for the rest of the first quarter. They held a 22-8 lead at the end of the first quarter and stretched that lead to 35-19 at the half.

Jimmy played as if he were in college and the rest of the players belonged in middle school. He was putting on a show for the nearly sold-out St. Louis Arena. In the first half he scored twenty points without missing a shot and collected nine rebounds. Bull pitched in with ten points and eight boards while Kenny added five assists.

Sleepy kept them fired up for the second half and they easily won the game 65-39, enabling Sleepy to replace his starters midway through the third period. All of the boys on the team played substantial minutes. When the game was finally over, Jimmy looked into the stands. He was surprised to see so many people cheering for the Eagles.

Sleepy estimated the crowd at 6,000. "Unbelievable for a ninth grade game," he mused to no one in particular. If Sleepy had known that Skits was going to publish another front page story the next day, he would not have been surprised that the rest of the games would be sold out.

As the players left the locker room, most of their parents were waiting for them. The parents had brought duffel bags of clothes and toiletries. Mrs. Feen had to work, so she packed a bag for both Jimmy and Jonesy and gave it to Kim, who was waiting with the parents. The players and their parents were talking about the game and the hotel and anything else that came to mind, when they heard Sleepy shout above all the chatter.

"Sorry to have to shout," he started, "but I need to get your attention. I would like to invite everyone for lunch at the hotel. If you don't know how to get there, follow the bus. Also, the players have to ride in the bus. See you at the hotel and thanks for coming to the game."

Kim handed Jimmy his bag. "I guess I'll see you tomorrow," she said.

"You're not coming to the hotel?" Jimmy asked.

"Well, I want to, but my parents are here."

Jimmy thought a moment. "Why don't you and your parents come to the hotel as my guests. I don't think it would be any problem at all."

This was one of the best things she liked about Jimmy, Kim realized. Even though it was an inconvenience for Jimmy to have her parents along, he knew it was something her parents wanted, so he sacrificed his wants for theirs. She was falling in love, but as her mom kept warning her, she was trying not to fall too fast.

Lunch went well. Everyone was joking and talking about the rest of the tournament. There were approximately fifty people gathered for the lunch. They ate in a private room Sleepy had reserved. After lunch, the team said goodbye to their guests and then Sleepy ordered his players to take a short nap and then be back in exactly one hour. They were going to scout the number one-rated team later in the afternoon.

The Eagles came away impressed. They understood why Chamberlain High School was ranked number one. They were good. Chamberlain manhandled their opponents by the score of 81-31. Sleepy made a mental note to ask the other coach why he ran the score up. This bothered Sleepy.

The team headed back to the hotel after the game. They ate dinner and then headed for their rooms. Sleepy reminded them that lights were to go out at 9:00 p.m. When the boys went up to their rooms it was only 7:30, so the players all retreated to Jimmy's and Jonesy's room and played video games, which Kenny had brought from home.

While his friends were playing video games, Jimmy called his mother. He told her all about the game and the hotel.

"Are you going to come to the game tomorrow?" he asked.

"I don't know yet, Jimmy. I have to wait and see if I can get someone to work my shift," Mrs. Feen answered her son.

"I hope you can come. The game starts at five."

"I'll try."

Sleepy came to the room at exactly nine o'clock. "Good game today, men," he said. "It's going to get a lot tougher in the next three games, so get your rest. Okay now, lights out." As he was leaving he told his players to meet him for breakfast at 8:00 a.m. The boys filed back to their separate rooms, leaving just Jonesy and Jimmy together for the first time all night.

Jimmy hit the light switch, but Jonesy called for him to turn it back on.

"What's up?" Jimmy asked as he turned the lights back on.

"I'll just be a quick minute. I have to call my brother," Jonesy explained to Jimmy as he dialed the phone. "I wanted to make sure he was going to come down to see the game tomorrow afternoon."

"Hello, who is this?" Jonesy asked, speaking very loudly into the phone. "Is this Ted?" he asked again and then abruptly, Jonesy hung up the phone. "The music was so loud I couldn't hear anything," Jonesy said to Jimmy. Jonesy laid down on his bed and stared at the ceiling.

Jimmy could tell his friend was really hurting inside, but he didn't know what to say. "Get some sleep, buddy," he finally said, trying to offer some encouragement. "We'll try again in the morning. We'll get hold of him somehow."

Jimmy had been friends with Jonesy since kindergarten. Jonesy, Ted and their father had moved to Jimmy's neighborhood from Chicago. Jimmy remembered Jonesy telling him that his mother had died when he was very young. Jimmy didn't press him for any details. Jonesy's father eventually got caught doing the wrong things and was sent to jail. Ted was already twenty years old, so he took custody of Jonesy and the two brothers were trying to make it by themselves.

Throughout his high school days, Ted was a star athlete. Built like a 180-pound concrete wall, Ted was as fast as anybody in the neighborhood. He was named to Parade's All-American Football Team at cornerback his senior year, but he turned down all the scholarship offers in order to stay with his brother.

Ted tried to find time to play football at the local junior college, but a part-time job didn't bring in enough money. He eventually dropped out of school and another promising career was over before it started. Ted tried to get a good paying job, but never found one he considered good enough. Eventually he took the easy way out and began selling drugs.

———

Jimmy and Jonesy met the rest of their teammates in the dining room the next morning. After eating some pancakes and eggs, the boys all returned to their rooms to get ready for the day. Sleepy had informed them that they were going to the Arena to watch the first game at 10:00 a.m., return to the hotel for lunch, catch a movie and then return to the Arena in time to prepare for their 5:00 p.m. game.

As soon as Jimmy and Jonesy were back in their room, Jonesy tried to call his brother again. After the third ring, Ted answered.

"Hello?"

"Ted, is that you?" Jonesy asked.

"Yeah bro, it's me. What's up? Did you guys win yesterday?"

"Yeah, we kicked butt. We have another game at five o'clock today. Are you coming?"

"Definitely, I'll be there," Ted answered. Jonesy could here some talking in the background. He wasn't sure, but it sounded like a group of people.

"Also," Jonesy added, "the team is having lunch in the hotel at noon. Why don't you come here and eat with us?"

"Yeah, that's cool too. I'll see you at noon." Ted hung up the phone, leaving Jonesy with a strange feeling.

"What's up?" Jimmy asked.

"He said he's coming today for lunch, but we'll see," Jonesy said skeptically.

"He'll show up," Jimmy assured his friend.

Bull, Willie and Kenny came into Jimmy's and Jonesy's room. Soon afterward, the rest of the team congregated in the room also. Bull had caught the tail end of the phone conversation with Jonesy and Ted.

"How's your brother doing?" Bull asked Jonesy. Most of the team knew that Ted was caught up in the drug scene. That was the way it was in their neighborhood. When somebody got messed up, everybody knew.

"I just wish he would get off that stuff. When he's high, he doesn't even seem like my brother. He seems like someone else."

"My brother's doing the same junk," Tommy Peterson said. "I know just what you mean."

These friends and teammates sat around and talked about the different things happening on the streets. It seemed as if each of them had a story that kids their age had no business knowing. However, each of the young men knew the streets were tough and that age didn't matter.

"You boys sure do know a lot for only being fifteen." The boys all whipped their heads around to see Sleepy standing in the doorway. He had been standing there, unnoticed, for the last ten minutes, listening to them talk. Sleepy surprised all the boys by taking a seat in the corner and sitting down.

"What were the streets like when you were growing up?" Bull asked Sleepy. "Were there as many guns as there are today?"

"No, not really," Sleepy answered after pausing a moment to think. "There were a few, but when I was your age, it was mostly knives and fists. You still had to watch what you were doing, but not as bad as today." The honesty at which Sleepy spoke impressed his players. Sleepy wasn't trying to glorify his old days or say it was harder or better when he was growing up. He was speaking from the heart and the boys saw this and appreciated it.

"I have a question for you guys," Sleepy said to everyone. "What should we, as a country, do to clean up this mess in the streets?"

"People need good jobs," Tommy said without hesitation. "Nobody is working and when they do find a job, it doesn't pay anything."

"I think the police need to lock up criminals longer," Bull said in a disgusted manner. "You got people shooting at each other and then they're back on the street in a few months. It isn't right. The only way to stop the violence is to lock up the criminals."

"The next Chief of Police, ladies and gentlemen," Kenny kidded Bull.

Everyone got a chuckle from that comment except Bull. Sleepy then surprised Jimmy by asking, "What do you think Jimmy?"

Jimmy had been listening to the conversation his friends were having, but he had not contributed to it up until this point. Now Sleepy was putting him on the spot. "I don't really know what should be done because I don't understand why or how people can do some of the things they do." Jimmy was scratching his ear with a confused look on his face. "I think the people who commit violent crimes think about themselves too much instead of thinking of others. They're just selfish." Jimmy was actually becoming a little mad at this point, mad at the people who were causing the violence and the drug abuse. He was mad at them for hurting his neighborhood and his country. The room was silent. Jimmy had put into words what everyone in the room was thinking. They all agreed with him.

"You're right, Jimmy," Sleepy said as he stood up. "Those people are selfish. When a person feels as if he can take someone else's life, greed has taken over. Selfish greed. They ought to be ashamed of themselves and we ought to punish them for doing it," Sleepy said in a cold manner. "Well boys," he stated, "these are serious problems that we have to think about. I like your attitudes. Now let's get ready to go to the Arena."

Even though the boys had become used to seeing Sleepy, they were once again aware of how lucky they were. He had a stature with which he carried himself that was very apparent as he talked with his team. The boys had idolized Sleepy when they hadn't known him. Now that they knew him, they strived to be like him even more.

The team met Sleepy downstairs and the whole group loaded into the bus and headed for the Arena. They watched a game between the third and the eleventh seeded teams. They watched up until halftime and then headed back to the hotel for lunch. It was now almost noon.

Many of the boys' parents, brothers and sisters met them for lunch. Sleepy had made it known that all family members were welcome any time. Jonesy saw Ted walk into the hotel and ask the desk clerk for information about where the team was. Ted looked like he had just got out of bed. His clothes were wrinkled and he looked dirty. Jonesy was embarrassed.

"Hello, nice to meet you. I was a big fan even before you started coaching my brother's team," Ted said when Jonesy introduced him to Sleepy. Ted was obviously thrilled to meet Sleepy and it showed in his voice.

Sleepy looked at Ted and could see the same things everyone else could. "This guy looks ragged," Sleepy thought to himself. Sleepy knew Ted's reputation because of his talk with Jonesy's teachers. He didn't doubt the drug reports.

"It's nice to meet you too," Sleepy finally answered. "You have a top-notch brother, I hope you're taking good care of him." Sleepy looked directly into Ted's eyes as he said this.

"I'm trying," Ted said. Ted knew he was lying as he said this. He knew he wasn't giving Jonesy a solid home life, but what could he do? Ted sat down at the long table and ate his lunch with all the others.

After lunch, the players headed to the movie theater for a matinee. After the movie, the boys went upstairs to their rooms and rested for forty-five minutes before heading to the Arena.

Sleepy had watched a video of one of their opponent's regular season games. They were good and Sleepy knew the Eagles would be in for a fight. The team was South West High and they were well balanced with speed and height. Sleepy did detect one weakness, namely ball handling. He focused on this ball-handling deficiency during his pre-game speech.

"Boys," he started, "there's no doubt in my mind that we can win this game today, but it's going to be tough. We have gotten used to blowing teams out this year, but it's not going to happen today. The team we are playing is good. However, we can beat them and we will beat them." Sleepy looked around the room and saw his players looking back at him confidently. He was pleased.

"The way to exploit them is to trap their ball handlers, forcing them to make errant passes. Our strength is defensive ability. You boys have a knack for knowing where the ball is going. If we can get them to throw the ball around, we can make some steals and get some easy points." Again, Sleepy looked around the room and again, he liked what he saw. His players were ready.

"We're going to do one thing different today, gentlemen. Bull, I'd like you and Jimmy to switch positions on our trap defense. Jimmy, you are to play the roving middle man while Bull will play the inbounder and chase the ball. We are going to do this for two reasons. Number one, I'd like to spread the trap defense from half-court to three-quarters court. Jimmy is better suited to picking off passes under these conditions. Number two, I want Bull to play the first pass very physically. Trap the first pass hard and force him into a bad pass. I'm not telling you to play dirty, but I think you can intimidate the other team's guards."

Sleepy drew a court on the blackboard and repeated what he had just said, explaining his changes one more time and also reviewing everyone else's positions. "Give it everything you've got," Sleepy reminded them. "Remember, the team is the most important thing." Sleepy began to raise his voice, pumping the players up. "I know you can win this game. All year long I've noticed something special about you boys. Not just the way you play basketball, but the way you treat one another. You care about each other. If you play basketball the same way, you can achieve greatness. Lose yourself in the game!" Sleepy took a deep breath. "Make the natural pass. Run the floor hard. Sweat. You can win. You can achieve your goals."

Sleepy was shouting by the end of his speech. The boys sprinted out of the locker room and onto the floor. Sleepy actually had to calm the boys down during warm-ups. They were all jumping as high and running as fast as they could. Sleepy figured from now on he had better save the emotional speech until right before tip-off.

The Eagles won the tip and immediately set up their triangle offense with Too Tall receiving the ball on the high block. Jimmy roamed the baseline looking for "alley oop" passes, backdoor cuts or quick passes in the corner. Kenny ran the top of the floor with Bull flashing across the middle and Jonesy looking for a soft spot in the weak side of the defensive in order to set himself for jump shots.

On defense, the team did just as Sleepy had instructed. Bull pressured the inbounds passer and then chased the ball from the backside, looking to trap the man along the sideline. Jimmy roamed the middle of the court, waiting for any long passes.

The plan worked well in the first quarter. Jimmy received three backdoor passes from Kenny and converted them all into baskets. One he finished with a reverse two-handed slam that had the sell-out crowd wondering how a boy so young could jump so high.

Mrs. Feen had finally taken a day off from work and was sitting in the stands watching her son for the first time all year. Kim and her parents sat with her. Mrs. Feen was seeing first-hand what she had been reading about in the papers all year long. Her son was an excellent player. When she heard people in the stands talk about how he was so good at such a young age, she felt pride well up inside. She knew how much he practiced and how determined he was. She knew he was earning it.

The Eagles led 20-14 at the end of the first quarter, but Bull had picked up two fouls, so Sleepy gave him a seat on the bench. Willie Stone replaced him. Willie was a good athlete, but he didn't have the quickness or the strength to match Bull. Sleepy eased the press from three-quarters court back to half-court because of this.

Sleepy also replaced Kenny with Junior. Kenny had a habit of getting out of control and Sleepy knew turnovers would be costly. Junior didn't have the physical quickness that Kenny had, but he was sure-handed and had the unshakable confidence of a heavyweight boxing champion.

Jonesy was off his mark in the first quarter, although he had gotten open shots, so Sleepy replaced him with Mark Abronovich in the second quarter. Mark was not the defensive player that Jonesy was, but his shooting from the outside was tops on the team.

The changes worked well on the offensive end. Mark hit two straight shots from the outside, both off low-risk chest passes from Junior. Willie Stone hit the boards hard and came up with an offensive rebound and put-back for two points. On defense however, the changes proved costly. Both Willie and Mark could not cover the floor as well as the starters, enabling South West to advance the ball with less pressure. South West took advantage of this by moving the ball methodically up the floor and then passing it into their center, who was having his way with Too Tall.

On defense, the South West players realized that Jimmy was as good as the papers had been saying and devoted two of their men to guard him. This strategy slowed the Eagles down and South West gradually pulled even and then slightly ahead. Sleepy decided to leave Bull on the bench the entire second quarter. High school was different from the NBA. Five fouls and Bull would have to sit out the rest of the game and Sleepy knew the team would need Bull's aggressiveness at the end. The Eagles went into the locker room six points down, 37-31.

During halftime, Sleepy reminded them of the need for pressure on the ball, all-out hustle and patience for the good shot. "Play as a team," he told them. As the second half was about to begin, Sleepy reinserted his starting five into the lineup.

The Eagles again jumped to a fast start with Bull applying much pressure and frustrating the smaller South West guards and forwards. Jimmy was all over the floor, stealing passes and converting them into lay-ins for himself and his teammates. By the end of the third quarter the Eagles had tied the score at 45.

The Eagles huddled around the bench between the third and fourth quarters. Sleepy saw the look of anxiousness on his player's faces. They had not been in a tight game like this for quite some time.

"We knew this was going to be a close game before it started, so don't worry. The team that wins this game is going to be the one that continues to be patient and sticks to the game plan. That team will be us," Sleepy said with supreme confidence. "The worst thing to do now is try to make the perfect pass or steal every ball. Remember, lose yourself in the game. If you challenge yourself to play the guy in front of you as hard and as smart as you can, then we'll win."

The buzzer signifying the start of the fourth quarter rang out. Sleepy looked at his boys as they were huddled around him. "I want everybody to look me in the eye right now and tell me you are going to play basketball the way it is meant to be played. No behind-the-back passes or selfish shots, just hard defense, boxing out for rebounds and hard cuts to the basket. This is basketball!" One referee made his way to the Eagles' huddle.

"Sleepy, we need your team on the floor," the referee warned.

Sleepy looked around at his team one last time. "Play as a team and win this game. Give me that commitment, play as a team. Play as a team!" Sleepy was sweating through his suit. He had lost himself in the game and his boys knew it. They could see the look in his eyes and they responded to it. The Eagles' starting five walked out onto the court for the start of the last quarter thinking not about girls or school or Friday nights. They were thinking about playing basketball. Sleepy had fired them up and focused their attention. The boys were set on carrying out their famous coach's will.

Despite his foul trouble, Bull played aggressively. He forced two turnovers in the first minute of the fourth quarter as the Eagles jumped out to a four-point lead. Jimmy scored both baskets, one on a driving lay-up and the other on a fifteen-foot jump shot. South West High fought back, but in the end the Eagles' defensive pressure was too much. The Eagles won the game by the score of 65-59. Sleepy was proud of his boys. They had played hard and had fought the whole game.

Sleepy was also proud of the players on the other team. They had also played hard, giving it a good run. Sleepy went over to the other coach and congratulated him on a game well played. One by one, Sleepy shook the hands of the South West High players. It was a great thrill for every one of them.

Sandra Phillips was surprised to see so many people waiting to see her husband. This was the first game she had attended all year and she hadn't expected so many of his fans to be here. She was well aware of his stature in the NBA, but she never figured it would carry over to a ninth grade tournament. She watched as Sleepy followed his bodyguards through the crowd of people. He smiled when he saw her and motioned for her to meet him in the bus.

Skits Cunningham was already on the bus, waiting for the team and Sleepy to arrive. Skits had blended into the surroundings well. At first, the players were a bit guarded around him. Lately however, they seemed to be acting natural, paying Skits little, if any attention. Skits liked it this way because he wanted to write about the relationships and the personalities of the teammates rather than just recapping the games.

Sleepy stepped up into the bus, with his wife close behind. He saw Skits sitting in one of the middle seats, pencil and paper in hand. Sleepy walked towards him and took a seat.

"Good game," Skits said.

"Thanks! The boys played real well today," Sleepy replied amiably. Sleepy looked at Skits and then asked, "Well, what do you think Skits? How good is Jimmy?"

"He's the best around here since you. Whether he will be better, only time will tell, but that boy sure can play."

———————————

Jonesy called his brother as soon as he returned to the hotel. He made arrangements to meet Ted after the next night's game. Ted was going to hang out with the team after the game. Jonesy hoped that being around Sleepy and the rest of the team would have a positive effect on Ted. He really hoped so.

CHAPTER XV

Calm Before The Storm

Jimmy had just gotten into bed when Sleepy poked his head into the room and said, "Lights out." Both Jimmy and Jonesy were tired, but neither one could fall right to sleep. They had too much on their minds.

Jonesy spoke into the darkness while lying face up on his bed. "Hey Jimmy, I've got to ask you a question."

"What is it, buddy?" Jimmy answered.

"It's about my brother. I was wondering if you thought he was a bad person?"

Jimmy thought seriously about the question and then answered the best he could. "I don't think he's bad, I just think he's, almost, like lost. You know what I mean?"

"I think you're right, I just wish I could do something about it," Jonesy said with a dejected voice.

"You can," Jimmy replied quickly, "you can talk to him and tell him that he's screwing up."

"He won't listen to me, you know that. He'll just tell me to stop worrying."

Jimmy didn't know how to reply because he knew Jonesy was right. Ted would not listen to his little brother. "I don't know what to tell you, Jonesy. Just try to be there when he needs you," Jimmy said as he gave his friend his best advice. It was a lot to think about for anyone, let alone two ninth graders.

———————————

By the time Kim showed up for lunch the next day, the team had already taken a stroll through the downtown. The boys were surprised to see people beeping their horns at them. Most people first recognized Sleepy and then figured out that the young men next to him were the Carver High Eagles they had been reading about in the newspapers. That didn't matter to the kids, however. They felt like Hollywood stars and were enjoying every minute of it.

Kim came up to Jimmy and kissed him on the cheek. He turned to see if the guys had seen this. They hadn't and he felt relieved. Jimmy liked Kim and liked her kissing him on the cheek, but his buddies had been giving him a hard time and Jimmy felt it was just as smart not to shove it in their faces.

There was a movie theater right next door to the hotel, so Jimmy and Kim decided to go see a movie after lunch. Jimmy asked Sleepy for permission first, of course.

"Be back by three. We're going to watch game films and then eat a light meal," Sleepy warned Jimmy.

"I'll be back, Coach."

Sleepy liked it when his players called him "Coach." Sleepy figured it was a good sign he was doing his job right. Bull and Jonesy joined Kim and Jimmy for the movie.

After the movie, the boys watched the game films while Kim went shopping in the mall near the hotel. After the game films, the team met for their pre-game snack. Many of the parents were already in the dining room. Again, Sleepy had invited his players' families and friends to come.

During the pre-game meal, conversation again centered on the troubles facing today's youth. Sleepy listened intently because he knew most of these kids lived with it every day. It wasn't a theoretical discussion between highbrow politicians or naive do-gooders. It was real life. Most of the parents felt as if there was nothing they could do, except move away from the trouble. Financial considerations usually prohibited this option though.

"That's why you boys should be trying to get scholarships. You can get good jobs and get away from the bad neighborhoods," Bull's father said to all of the players.

"Yes, I agree with you Mr. McKinnon," Sleepy said, "but the way to do that is not through sports, but through education. Only a small percentage of kids go to college because of sports. So in turn, there's a greater chance of going to college because of good academics than good athletics."

"You're right, Mr. Phillips, but in real life something entirely different happens," a new voice said. Willie Stone's mother was a guidance counselor at the middle school and had been working with kids for many years. She was speaking from the heart. "What really happens is that athletics, rather than good, solid studying, is promoted as the way out. Athletic scholarships are viewed with great interest, whereas academic scholarships are ignored, or in some cases, cause for ridicule. Until academics and schoolwork are viewed as just as important as athletics, we have little chance of improving the situation."

Everyone debated the issue a while longer. Sleepy was happy that his boys sat there and listened. He wanted them in a serious mood.

Ted had told Jonesy that he would come to the hotel again, but he never showed. Jonesy didn't want to make a big deal out of it, but Jimmy could tell he felt things were spiraling out of control for his brother. Jimmy was mentally challenging himself to concentrate on the game, but it was hard. His buddy's brother was in trouble and he didn't know how to help.

Sleepy looked his boys over and figured they were antsy to get to the game. Even though it was only a little after 4:30 p.m., Sleepy herded his team onto the bus. Sleepy didn't think being a little early would adversely affect their play. If truth be told, Sleepy was a little antsy himself.

The team went directly to the locker room once they reached the Arena. The other quarterfinal game had been played earlier in the afternoon leaving the floor empty. Some of the players put on their warm-up gear and headed to the court for some practice shooting. They were surprised to see the stands already half full. There was no doubt that Sleepy and his Carver High Eagles were the fan favorites. After twenty minutes of shooting, Sleepy called the boys back into the locker room for some last minute instructions.

Sleepy focused more on the players' frame of mind than on strategy. Sleepy wanted to give them some motivation. He thought about the earlier conversations they had had about the problems in their neighborhoods. He called the boys into a tight circle.

"We've almost achieved our goals," Sleepy said to them first. "We've played well and now we have three games left to finish the season undefeated." The players were all listening intently, ready for Sleepy's fiery speech. "But let me tell you.

Don't go thinking you've done anything yet. Our goal was for an undefeated season and we're not there yet. There's work to be done." Sleepy stood silently, letting his statement sink in to the players.

"Do you remember the conversation we've been having about all the troubles in our neighborhoods?" he asked his players as he continued his speech. They nodded their heads to indicate they did remember. "The real problem is we have a bunch of work to do, but not enough people doing it. More people need to tell little kids it's better to be smart than to jump high. Hard work in the classroom isn't being rewarded like hard work on the basketball floor. Let me tell you something fellas, it isn't going to get any better until somebody puts his nose down and does the work. There might not be the glory if you do it that way, but at least the person doing the work has the satisfaction of knowing that he did it." Sleepy could tell he had confused his players.

"The same thing goes here today," he said loudly. "I don't want to hear about our losing after this game and how bad we feel. I don't want to hear it. You know why, because there is work to do and if you do it, we'll win. If you don't do it, we'll lose. Simple! Put your nose down and sweat. Put your nose down and box out. Put your nose down and steal the ball. Put your nose down and lose yourself in the game of basketball. Play it like you know how. Out-hustle the other team. Harass them on defense. Beat them on offense. Put your nose down and with no excuses you can say you gave it everything you had."

Sleepy was out of breath. He had lost control and went overboard he thought. But as he looked at his players he realized he had touched a nerve with them. They realized they needed to put their noses down to win this game. Nobody said a word. The team was sitting there like a volcano ready to erupt. Jimmy finally stood up.

"Coach, can we hit the floor?"

"Yes," Sleepy replied. The players then walked out of the room. There were no high fives or laughing. The players walked to the floor with their noses down, ready to go to work.

"Have you seen Ted yet?" Jonesy asked Jimmy as they were doing their pre-game lay-up drills.

"I haven't seen him," Jimmy answered.

Jonesy looked into the family section of the bleachers, but he didn't see his brother. Jimmy noticed how preoccupied Jonesy was with his brother's absence. Jimmy scolded his friend, "Don't worry, he'll be here. Besides, there's nothing you can do until after the game, so focus on the game." Jonesy knew that Jimmy was right.

From the opening tip it was clear that their opponents were badly outmatched. The Eagles had both the height and quickness advantage, propelling them to an easy, 67-48 victory. Excellent performances by Bull and Kenny carried the team, but Jimmy and Jonesy had their worst games of the year. In the locker room after the game, Bull overheard Jonesy asking Jimmy about Ted. Bull butted right in.

"What's up with you two. You've been whispering all day and you didn't have your heads in the game. If you two play like that tomorrow, we're going home losers. So what gives?"

"Well Bull," Jonesy said honestly, "I'm worried about my brother. He's all messed up right now. He was supposed to be here and he didn't show."

Bull felt terrible. He hadn't realized Jonesy was worrying about family. "I'm sorry. I shouldn't have said anything."

"No, you're right," Jonesy replied. "I have to concentrate on the game when we're on the floor. Coach is right when he says you have to lose yourself in the game." Jimmy nodded his head in agreement.

"Thank goodness you fellas played a whale of a game because Jonesy and I sure didn't," Jimmy added truthfully.

The boys finished their showers and got dressed. The music was turned up and the laughter started, but Jimmy, Bull and Jonesy were each deep in their own thoughts. Each of them knew friends or relatives caught up in the bad side of their neighborhood. They also knew that before too long, the bad side always caught up with them.

Sleepy was not only a great player and a good coach, but he was also an observant man. He knew there was something wrong with his star player the minute the game began. Jimmy was usually the first to dive to the floor or fight ferociously for a loose ball, but tonight he was a little off. Sleepy had noticed Jimmy looking into the stands quite often. He knew that Kim had been hanging around lately. Sleepy didn't know if she was the problem, but he was going to get to the bottom of this. Jimmy had to be one hundred-percent if the Eagles were going to win this tournament.

The team headed for the bus, stopping only long enough to tell friends and family to meet them at the hotel for breakfast at 8:00 the next morning. Bull, Jimmy and Jonesy all looked for Ted, but he wasn't to be found. However, Jonesy did spot one of Ted's close friends, James Washington.

Jonesy, Jimmy and Bull walked directly towards James. "Great game, fellas," James said as he saw them approach.

Jonesy cut him off quickly. "Where's my brother?"

"I don't know man, he didn't show up," James answered evasively. Bull was becoming impatient.

"James, follow the bus to the hotel. We need to talk with you." Bull said this as an order rather than a request. Even though James was older, he didn't want to mess with Bull, so he obliged.

"I got somewhere to go, but I can do that," James answered, acting indifferent. When the team arrived at the hotel, Jimmy, Bull and Jonesy got off in a hurry and headed towards James, who was already in the lobby. The three boys asked a lot of questions, but James knew nothing about where Ted was.

Sleepy watched his three players carefully. He wasn't sure what was going on, but he knew he had better keep an eye on them. It was nearing 9:00 p.m., so Sleepy sent the players to their rooms. The semi-final game was the next night at 7:00 p.m. and Sleepy wanted them well rested for it.

Around 10:00 p.m., the phone rang in Jimmy's and Jonesy's room, waking both boys from a deep sleep. Jonesy was closest to the phone so he picked it up. "Yeah, is that you Ted? Where are you? No, no, that's all right. I was just worried something was up. Yeah, we won. The game tomorrow will be at seven o'clock. Okay, I'll see you here."

"What's up?" Jimmy asked as soon as Jonesy hung up the phone.

"He called to apologize for missing the game. He said he had a couple of things to do, but he would be here tomorrow to meet us before the game."

"Is that it?" Jimmy asked, expecting more insight from his friend.

"Jimmy, he just doesn't seem right," Jonesy answered. "I don't know. I really don't know." Jimmy could hear the sadness in his friend's voice. Jimmy had his mother, but Jonesy didn't have any parents living with him.

Jimmy felt bad for his friend, but he was determined not to let the same thing happen to him tomorrow as had happened today. He was still concerned about Ted, but he wasn't going to let it affect his game. He wasn't going to look into the stands even a single time. Jimmy told himself that he would worry after the game.

Jimmy played the next night as if he had taken his own advice. By the time the first quarter had ended, Jimmy had fifteen points, three blocked shots and three high-flying slam dunks. The packed house got what they came for. The freshman phenom was ready to play. The Eagles held a twenty-five point lead at the half and it got no closer the rest of the way.

As the boys hit the showers, Jimmy asked Jonesy if he had seen Ted. Ted had not shown up at the hotel before the game and Jimmy was wondering if Jonesy had seen him in the stands.

"Nope. I haven't seen him," Jonesy replied with a hurt look.

Jimmy didn't want to pry too deeply right now. Most of the guys on the team knew what was going on. They had known Ted for a long time, as Jimmy had. They also knew Ted was getting mixed up with the wrong crowd. Each of the boys felt bad for Jonesy.

———————————

Kim and her parents were waiting for Jimmy after the game. Mrs. Feen had been unable to come because of her work schedule, but she had managed to get the next day off in order to watch the championship game. Kim could tell Jimmy was in a strange mood, but she didn't know why. She thought he should have been in a great mood after winning the game. When she left the hotel around 8:00 p.m., she was still wondering what was wrong.

By the time the boys headed for their rooms for the night, Jonesy and Jimmy had given up on Ted. Jonesy figured he was out "doing some errands," as Ted called it, but both Jonesy and Jimmy knew that meant delivering drugs. Jonesy had not been able to put his brother out of his mind during the game and it showed in his play. Sleepy had replaced him with Mark Abronovich early in the first quarter and Jonesy received only a few minutes after that.

Other than for the situation with Jonesy's brother, the Eagles were in high spirits. They had advanced to the final game of the tournament and were set to play Chamberlain, the number-one-rated team. The Eagles were looking forward to the chance to prove who was really number one.

———————————

Sleepy hadn't felt this good in a long time. Ever since he had retired from professional basketball the competition that had driven him his entire life was missing, but he had found it again in the old George Washington Carver High School gymnasium. These kids had revived him. These were "his kids" now. He felt a responsibility towards them. Sleepy laughed to himself at his situation. Here he was a world-famous sports celebrity and he was choosing to coach a ninth grade basketball team. "Isn't life grand," he thought.

CHAPTER XIV

Busted

Sleepy made his rounds of all the rooms, warning his players that "lights out" was in thirty minutes. All the boys were in their rooms relaxing and that made Sleepy proud. Many kids their age would have been fooling around, but his boys were getting ready to win.

Jonesy told Jimmy that he was going down to the lobby for a few minutes to get a Sports Illustrated and a glass of orange juice.

"You want anything Jimmy?"

"No thanks, and you had better hurry. If Sleepy catches you out past nine, he's going to give it to you," Jimmy warned his friend.

As soon as Jonesy had stepped out of the room, the phone rang. It was Ted.

"Hello, Jimmy, is that you?" Ted asked in a rush.

"Yeah, it's me."

Bull had just happened to walk into the room when the phone rang and watched as Jimmy's face took a concerned look. All Jimmy was saying was, "Yes, yes, I understand," and then "how much?" Bull was curious about who Jimmy was talking with.

When Jimmy hung up the phone Bull quizzed him. Jimmy told him that the caller was Ted and that he was at Pepper Brown's house. "Ted owes Pepper three hundred dollars and he doesn't have it. The problem is, Pepper is demanding the money now."

Pepper Brown was one of the drug dealers in Jimmy's and Bull's neighborhood. Jimmy and Bull had never actually met Pepper before, they just knew of him and had seen him on the street a couple of times. The word around town was that it was not a good idea to owe Pepper money. He wasn't a nice guy and somebody usually got hurt.

"Well, what are you going to do?" Bull asked.

"He asked me to loan him the money," Jimmy replied.

"Are you going to do it?"

"Yep, and I'm going to give it to him tonight."

"What did you say?" Bull exclaimed. Bull was concerned that Jimmy was getting too deep in this. "Maybe you better wait and see what Jonesy says," Bull cautioned him.

"I can't. I promised Ted I wouldn't tell Jonesy."

Bull didn't know what to say. He knew the best thing was for Jimmy to stay out of Ted's mess, but Bull knew that Jimmy had made up his mind to help and he would not be able to talk him out of it. "Okay," Bull said, "If you're going, then I'm going with you."

Jimmy tried to dissuade Bull, but Bull was having none of it. He had made up his mind and that was that. If Bull wanted to go, it was fine with him Jimmy reasoned. Besides, Jimmy felt better with Bull watching his back anyway.

"Let's get out of here," Jimmy said as he grabbed his jacket. "We'll call a taxi with the spending money Sleepy gave us, then stop at my house to get my checkbook and then head to Pepper's house. We should be back by ten-thirty, no problem."

"What are you going to tell Jonesy?" Bull asked.

"I'll think of something on the way back. Now let's get out of here before he comes back."

Bull and Jimmy ran to the end of the hallway and took the steps downstairs so they wouldn't see Jonesy on the elevator. They snuck outside through one of the back doors, walked around to the front of the hotel and hailed a cab.

When Jonesy got back to the room he was surprised that Jimmy wasn't there. It was already 8:50 p.m., only ten minutes before "lights out." Jonesy figured Jimmy had gone downstairs or to another room. He fell onto his bed and went to sleep right away.

The blowing wind woke Jonesy from his sleep about an hour after his head had hit the pillow. He was surprised to see Jimmy still missing. Jonesy opened the door and looked down the hallway. No sign of Coach Phillips. Jonesy figured Jimmy might be in Bull's and Willie's room, so he checked. He knocked lightly on the door and after a few moments Willie opened it.

"Is Jimmy in there with you guys?"

"No, I'm the only one here. I don't know where Bull is either." Both boys were missing a roommate. Jonesy had no idea what was going on. He went back to his own room and lay awake in bed, staring at the clock.

As the cab approached Pepper's house, Jimmy and Bull tensed up. They were both scared and both knew it. "We'll go in, give them the check and get Ted out of there. We'll drop him off and head straight back to the hotel," Bull suggested.

"I agree," Jimmy said nervously.

The cab driver had been listening to the boys talk the whole ride. He was concerned they were getting into something that was none of their business. "Are you boys sure you need to go in there?" the cabbie asked both of them. "This house don't look so good. I've been listening to you talk about getting your friend out, but you had better make sure *you* can get out."

Jimmy listened intently to the old cabbie. "Don't worry sir, we'll be back out in five minutes." The cabbie shook his head and muttered something under his breath.

Bull and Jimmy got out of the car and walked toward the house. The house had a small chain link fence around the outside and the grass looked like it hadn't been cut in four weeks. There was a large dog chained to a tree in the side yard and another barking loudly from the back of the house.

Jimmy and Bull opened the small gate and walked by the dog, who just turned its head and looked at them. When they were about ten feet from the house, a voice called out.

"Don't come no closer. Who's there?"

"Jimmy Feen. I'm here to talk to Ted Jones."

The voice in the night laughed loudly. "Hey Pepper, the superstar is here," Jimmy heard him say.

"Come on in," the boys heard someone else say.

As the boys stepped into the house, they didn't expect what they saw. Instead of the old, run-down house that it looked like from the outside, Pepper lived in style. There was a huge, state-of-the-art stereo and a giant-screen television. Pepper had expensive things all about the house. Jimmy and Bull both knew where the money came from so they were not impressed. Sitting around the room were a couple of girls and about five or six guys. Everybody there seemed to be twenty-one or twenty-two. Ted was sitting in the corner on a sofa chair. He didn't look very good.

"So who do we give the money to?" Bull said abruptly, wanting to get out of there as quickly as possible.

"Me," Pepper said as he stepped towards the boys. Pepper had a mustache and wasn't wearing a shirt. He was definitely in good shape and was smiling broadly. He stood with his hand out to both Jimmy and Bull. They shook his hand, although warily. Pepper laughed. "Don't be scared of me. I'm not the reason you're here, Ted is. I just want to wish you fellas good luck tomorrow." Jimmy and Bull were both caught off-guard. They had expected a hard time, but instead Pepper was as nice as could be.

"Okay Pepper," Jimmy said. "Here's your check for three hundred."

"A check," Pepper laughed loudly. "I don't normally accept checks, but I guess I can make an exception this time. Just lay it on the table over there. I trust you two." Pepper was still standing in front of the two boys. "How is it to play for Sleepy Phillips?" he asked, changing the subject. "He was my idol growing up."

Jimmy answered him. "It's been great. He's a great coach and a great guy, but we have to leave now. We're breaking curfew."

"No problem fellas, I'm not offended," Pepper said casually. "Just remember, if you get caught, it was Ted's fault - not mine. If he would have paid me the money when he was supposed to, you wouldn't have had to be here. Isn't that right, Ted?" Ted looked up from his seat and nodded his head in agreement.

Everyone in the neighborhood knew that Pepper Jones was the main drug dealer around. Not only did the neighborhood folks know it, but the police knew it too. By the worst of unlucky circumstances, Jimmy and Bull were at Pepper's house on the very night the police had been preparing a raid.

Jimmy looked out the window as he, Bull and Ted were about to leave, but he didn't see the cab. He became worried. Jimmy was opening the door when, with a blaze of blinding light, he heard a voice booming directly towards him.

"GET DOWN ON THE GROUND WITH YOUR ARMS STRAIGHT ABOVE YOU. GET DOWN! GET DOWN!" Jimmy stood there in shock. He did not comprehend what was happening. He watched, still as a scarecrow, as the police rushed towards him. He barely felt a thing as the police wrestled him to the ground. He was too stunned to notice the same thing happening to Bull.

As soon as Pepper and his friends heard the police, they turned off all the lights and ran for the back yard. Police cars swarmed into Pepper's yard and driveway. Luckily, no shots were fired. The police came out the front door with Pepper and four of his friends. Jimmy and Bull watched the entire proceedings from the back of a squad car. Jimmy waited to see Ted come out of the house, but he never did. The police ushered everyone into police cars and took them downtown to the police station.

"I can't believe this. Man, we're done," Bull said, seething with anger, but Jimmy didn't say anything. He only looked out the window and thought about how he had gotten himself and his best friend into this mess and how he was going to get them out of it.

_____

Everyone at the hotel was in bed, except for Jonesy, Willie, and of course, Jimmy and Bull. Jonesy had no idea where his two friends were. He was mulling over all of the possibilities when the phone rang. Jonesy looked at the clock and it read 1:30 a.m.

"Hello."

"Jonesy, it's Ted." Ted then explained the whole story to his little brother. Ted explained how he had run out the back, jumped the fence and sprinted home, but Jimmy and Bull were taken downtown. Jonesy was flabbergasted. He hadn't even known that Ted had called Jimmy for help in the first place.

"I can't believe you got my friends involved in your mess," Jonesy said in an angry tone. "This is ridiculous. How can you do this? If you want to mess up your own life go ahead, but leave me and my friends alone."

Ted knew Jonesy was going to react like this, but it didn't make him feel any better. When you're the older brother and your younger brother is lecturing you, it is a humbling experience. Ted realized as he listened to Jonesy say hurtful things that he had to change or he and his brother would never be close again. Jonesy finally hung up the phone in disgust.

_____

The police were having a good time at the station. They had busted a known drug dealer with dope, guns and money at the house, together with seven of his friends. Each member of the police force knew that the war on drugs was fought one day at a time. They were happy to win this battle without any violence, which was always a possibility when dealing with street punks.

Sergeant McMichael was sitting in his chair reading the paper when the people from Pepper Brown's house were being booked. The St. Louis police station was a series of large open rooms. A few officers had just finished their shifts and were unwinding, including McMichael. He was sitting at his desk, reading the sports page and drinking a cup of coffee. He wasn't paying much attention to the bust being done right in front of him.

He began to read an article by Skits Cunningham about the Carver High Eagles and their famous coach. The article talked about the tournament, the undefeated season and the chance meeting between Jimmy and Sleepy that started it all. After reading the whole article, McMichael started up a conversation with his partner, Thomas Jackson. Jackson was busy typing up a report.

"These kids are supposed to be pretty good," McMichael said to Jackson.

"Who?" Jackson answered, hardly paying attention to his partner.

"The kids playing for Sleepy Phillips."

"Yeah, they are good. That Feen boy, they say he's the best in this area since Sleepy played high school ball. I went to see them play last night. It was a lot of fun. The Arena was packed."

"That's what the paper says. But it also says that if it wasn't for Sleepy, there wouldn't even be a ninth grade tournament," McMichael stated.

Jackson nodded, "Probably right, but..." and Jackson did not say another word. When he looked up to finish his statement to his partner, Jimmy happened to be right beside him. Jackson's eyes met Jimmy's.

"Are you going to the game tomorrow afternoon?" McMichael asked his partner, not realizing it was past midnight already. Jackson did not answer.

"Hey buddy, are you going to the game tomorrow night?" he asked again. Still, Jackson didn't answer. Finally, McMichael looked up from the paper to see what his partner was doing. Pretty soon he was doing the same thing: staring right at Jimmy Feen.

"Hey, you're the kid from Sleepy's team," McMichael stated.

Jonesy knew what he had to do. He had to walk up to Coach Phillips' door, wake him up and tell him exactly what had happened. However, as Jonesy was learning, doing the right thing isn't always easy. Jonesy could barely make his legs move. Even though it was his brother, Ted, who had caused this whole mess, Jonesy felt responsible. He was about to open his door when the phone rang again. It was Bull.

"Jonesy, it's Bull. Jimmy and I are at the police station and...," but before Bull could finish, Jonesy cut him off and told Bull that he knew everything. Bull told Jonesy not to say anything to Sleepy yet and to wait by the phone for further instructions. Before Jonesy could offer his apologies, Bull hung up the phone.

Sergeants McMichael and Jackson waited for Bull to hang up the phone and then began to ask questions. The two detectives had separated Bull and Jimmy from the rest of the group. Jackson started the questioning.

"Are you two boys into drugs?"

"No sir," both Jimmy and Bull responded in tandem.

"Then what in the world were you doing at a drug house at eleven o'clock at night? You even have a game tomorrow," Jackson added, not concealing his disgust. Jimmy didn't answer. He knew he had done nothing wrong and he also knew he wasn't going to rat on Jonesy's brother, even though he had every right.

"Well boys, are you going to answer the question?" McMichael asked impatiently.

"We were just helping someone out," Bull finally responded.

Jackson had a confused look on his face. These two boys looked like good kids, but for some reason they didn't want to explain what had happened. "Frankly, that answer isn't good enough," Jackson grumbled at Bull. "If I don't get some details, you two are going to get booked with the rest of your distinguished group."

Bull understood the police officer's threat. A long time ago, Bull's older brother had been turned down for a good job because of an arrest record. Bull knew this would stay on both his and Jimmy's records and he didn't want that to happen. Besides, it really was Ted's fault.

"I'll tell you what happened," Bull said as he decided not to get arrested for Ted. Jimmy flashed Bull a disapproving look. Bull's eyes met Jimmy's and Bull began to think again. "I'll tell you what I told you last time. We were just trying to get someone out of trouble." Bull had conceded to Jimmy's wishes for silence. Jimmy just turned his head and looked at the ceiling as Bull said this. Jackson and McMichael told Bull and Jimmy to stay seated. The officers walked to the other side of the room.

"What do you think?" Jackson asked after they were sure the two boys couldn't hear.

"I've seen a lot of druggies and punks in my day and these boys look like neither," McMichael answered.

"I know what you mean," Jackson added. Just then a clerk came to the sergeants and told them that a cab driver wanted to make a statement about the drug bust.

"It's about the two boys you've been talking to," she informed them.

The cab driver told the officers that he had overheard Jimmy and Bull talking about paying off a friend's debt to get him out of trouble. McMichael and Jackson had each seen enough trash in the last twenty years on the force to know the importance of helping good kids. Both sergeants made up their minds to help these two boys any way possible. They decided not to book them as accessories, but to release them into Sleepy Phillips' custody. McMichael asked Jackson to hand him the sports page.

"I think the article said the team was staying in a hotel downtown. Yeah, here it is," he said as he looked at the newspaper article. Jackson called information and got the hotel's phone number and then dialed the number. It was now 3:30 a.m.

Sergeant Jackson couldn't convince the front desk clerk that he was not a crank caller. Finally, the clerk had his manager talk to Jackson. Again, Jackson explained the situation to the manager. The manager explained that he would hang up the phone and dial the police station and ask for Jackson. This would prove to the manager that Jackson was not a crank caller.

The switchboard operator forwarded the call to Jackson and the manager was satisfied. The front desk rang Sleepy's room phone with Jackson waiting on the other end. After approximately ten rings, Sleepy picked up the phone and in a groggy voice asked, "Who in the world is this?"

"Sergeant Jackson of the St. Louis Police Department. Sorry to have to call you so late, Mr. Phillips, but we have a couple of your players down here and we wanted to call you before we did anything."

Sleepy woke up quickly. "My players, who are you talking about?"

"Jimmy Feen and William McKinnon."

"Jimmy and Bull," Sleepy said out loud in disbelief. "What's the matter? Is anything wrong? Are they okay?"

"They're in good health, but they were mixed up in a bit of trouble and we knew you were their coach, so we gave you a call," Sergeant Jackson responded.

"What do you want me to do?" Sleepy asked.

"I was thinking you might want to come down to the station and pick these boys up. We haven't booked them yet so there's no record of their being here..."

"I'll be there in twenty minutes," Sleepy interrupted him. Sleepy still didn't know what had happened or why the boys were at the station, but it seemed the police were going to let them go without a big deal. Sleepy called downstairs and requested that a cab be made ready for him. He put on a warm-up suit over his pajamas and dashed down the stairs.

———————————

Skits Cunningham had never been a sound sleeper. He was always thinking about his next column. Being a journalist, Skits was on the road a lot and during these sleepless nights he would roam the lobbies looking for a good magazine or newspaper. These sleepless nights never really bothered him though. Skits knew the good stories did not always come between the hours of 9:00 a.m. and 5:00 p.m.

Most of this night Skits had been reading the current issue of *Sports Illustrated*. However, at about 3:45 a.m., he got an urge for a candy bar so Skits headed down to the hotel lobby. He gave the vending machine his seventy-five cents and was about to get back on the elevator when he saw Sleepy Phillips jog down the stairs and head for the front desk. Skits checked his watch and it read exactly 3:50 a.m. Skits' investigative juices began to flow. When he saw a cab pull up and Sleepy rush toward it, Skits knew there was a story in all of this.

Skits ran over to the front counter, "Do you have any rental cars available?"

"Not this late, sorry sir," was the reply from the desk clerk. Skits ran out the front door in time to see Sleepy's cab pull off. Skits looked around the parking lot. He needed a car so he could follow Sleepy. Out of the corner of his eye Skits saw what looked to be a maid get into her car. Skits ran to her.

"Hello, my name is Skits Cunningham. I'm a reporter for the *Times* and I need to use your car. I'll give you one hundred dollars to use it for the rest of the night."

"You probably want to follow Sleepy Phillips, don't you?" asked the maid, who had also seen Sleepy run out of the hotel and into a cab.

"Two hundred and yes I do," Skits negotiated.

"How about three hundred and I'll drive?"

"You have a deal."

Skits climbed into the passenger seat and they hurried off to catch sight of the cab carrying Sleepy.

"So what are you going to do with us?" Bull asked the two officers.

"We're not going to do anything with you," McMichael said with slight amusement. Jimmy and Bull gave each other puzzled looks.

"We figured we couldn't be tough enough on you so we called your coach. He should be here any minute," Jackson said with a huge smile. Jimmy and Bull both slumped in their chairs.

Word had gotten out at the police station that Sleepy was coming. Because it was so late, not many people were there, but he still had to sign a few autographs and shake a few hands as he walked in through the front door. The receptionist showed him to a room where Sergeants Jackson and McMichael were waiting.

"First of all, I'm sorry that we have to meet in a situation like this," Jackson said, obviously excited to meet Sleepy. "We believe your boys were not involved in any criminal activity.

Looks like they were in the wrong place at the wrong time. They say they were helping someone, but they haven't explained any more than this."

Sleepy was a little confused. "Are they in any trouble with the law?" he asked.

"No sir, that's why we called you. It seems to us that you could do a better job of making an impression on them than we could."

Sergeant McMichael had been listening and nodding his head in agreement. "Mr. Phillips," McMichael interjected, "we've been following your team the whole season and it seemed like you had a nice bunch of kids. So, when we found these kids in a drug bust, it didn't sit well. We're pretty sure they were just helping someone out of a jam, but they won't give us any information. However, they seem like good kids so we're going to let them walk with you."

"They are good kids," Sleepy confirmed. "I thank you for letting them go and you can bet I'll make a lasting impression."

"Very good then," Jackson said. "We'll send the boys to the front desk. You can wait for them there if you like."

"Thank you very much for going easy on them," Sleepy said, meaning every word.

As Sleepy waited for his two best players to be led out of the station, his eye caught a sudden movement by the door. Sleepy shook his head in disbelief as he saw Skits Cunningham making his way into the police station. Sleepy's eyes met Skits'.

Jimmy and Bull came walking out with Detective Jackson at their side. When they saw Sleepy standing there, both put their heads down. They couldn't look him in the eyes. Sleepy didn't say a word to them. He walked out to the cab with the boys close behind. As he passed Skits on the way out, Sleepy invited him to have breakfast at 8:00 a.m..

"My pleasure," Skits responded.

Not a single word was spoken in the cab ride back to the hotel. Jimmy and Bull got out of the cab and followed Sleepy to the hotel entrance. Without saying a word to either of the boys, Sleepy walked to the elevator and got in, the boys followed. When the elevator reached their floor, Sleepy went directly to his room and shut the door, still without saying a word. It was 5:00 a.m.

When Jimmy walked into his room, Jonesy was still awake. "Jimmy, Ted called and told me everything. I'm really sorry that you got caught up in my problems. I'm really sorry," Jonesy said with true emotion.

"It's all right, buddy. We've been friends so long that your problems are my problems. I'm going to get some sleep now. We'll talk about it in the morning."

"Hello Skits," Sleepy said as he sat down at the breakfast table in the corner of the hotel restaurant. Skits had been reading the newspaper while he waited for Sleepy.

"Good morning. Some night last night."

"Yes it was," Sleepy said without a smile. "I'm wondering how you knew I was at the police station."

"Quite simple," Skits replied. "I saw you leave at four in the morning so I knew something was up. I followed you to the police station because you're the biggest sports story in the nation and your undefeated Eagles are the biggest story in St. Louis."

"Yes, I've been seeing that, but don't you think that's a little much for a bunch of ninth grade kids? Most of them aren't even going to make the varsity next year."

"Maybe you're right," Skits answered with a point of introspection, "but Jimmy Feen is going to be a fine player. Definitely major college material and then maybe the NBA." Sleepy didn't reply, but he agreed with Skits. After a few minutes of awkward silence, Sleepy got down to business.

"Skits, I want to level with you. Not as a celebrity to a journalist, but man to man. I took this job not because of the publicity but because of the kids. I've grown very fond of these boys and I don't want to see anything but positive things happen to them. If you print a story about how Jimmy and Bull ended up in jail last night, then all the good things they've done this season will be overshadowed. I don't want that to happen."

"First of all," Skits responded, "I don't know exactly what happened, but I'm sure I could find out." Sleepy had known Skits long enough to know that was true. "I'm a journalist and this is my story. If these boys can't play today then everybody is going to ask why. I have to write about it or someone else surely will."

Sleepy moved uncomfortably in his seat. "I don't agree. If the boys don't play and everyone believes it was because they were sick, then there's no problem." Again, Sleepy moved awkwardly in his chair. Sleepy was in a strange position because he had not talked to the boys yet and he too wasn't quite sure what had exactly happened.

"I don't know if I can do that Sleepy," Skits said honestly.

Sleepy looked down at his plate of food. "Skits," he said without looking up, "If you don't print anything about those two boys being at the police station, I'll give you an exclusive story the whole country will want to know about."

Skits' interest perked up. "What do you mean? What kind of story?"

"It has to do with my professional plans for next year," Sleepy tempted him. "I'll announce it one week from today. If you protect Jimmy and Bull then I'll give you an exclusive interview."

"I have to know what it's about," Skits tried to demand.

"Sorry Skits, that's my offer." With that, Sleepy got up from the table and went to meet his team. The team was already in the main cafeteria eating breakfast when Sleepy walked in. Each of the boys knew that Bull and Jimmy were in trouble, so the mood was very somber.

Sleepy didn't say a word as the players ate breakfast. After they were done, they went to their rooms, packed their bags and got ready to check out of the hotel. They were heading home directly after the game.

The team arrived at the Arena at 10:00 a.m., two hours before tip-off. As the team entered the building it seemed as if the entire city was waiting for them. Banners were hanging everywhere. Cheerleaders were milling around the sidelines and the consolation game was being played before a sellout crowd. It seemed as if all 8,000 people had come to root for Sleepy Phillips and his Carver High Eagles.

Sleepy joined his team in their reserved seats to watch the first half of the consolation game. As soon as the other teams left the locker rooms after halftime, the Eagles made their way in. Sleepy didn't join them.

"What in the heck happened to you two last night," Kenny nearly shouted as the locker room door closed behind the team. It was the first time the players had been alone all morning.

"I don't want to talk about it," Bull muttered with his head down.

"How about you Jimmy, do you want to tell us what's up?" Tommy questioned.

"I really don't," Jimmy answered. "However, I do want to apologize to everyone. I'm sorry that I broke curfew."

The players went to their lockers and began to dress for the game. Jimmy and Bull were not surprised to see that their assigned lockers were empty. There were no uniforms hanging for them to wear. The other players also noticed that Jimmy's and Bull's uniforms were missing.

"This isn't fair. You guys were just trying to help. It wasn't your fault, it was mine," Jonesy said to his friends. He was upset, but quieted down as Sleepy walked in.

"Boys, I have an announcement to make. Last night Bull and Jimmy broke curfew. I'm sure you all know this already. This was in direct violation of the rules we agreed upon before coming to this tournament. I have to say that I'm extremely disappointed that it happened, but as your coach I have to act responsibly. I would like to give Jimmy and Bull one chance to explain what happened."

Jimmy looked at Sleepy. Sleepy could see Jimmy's eyes tearing up, but the young man offered no explanation. Bull looked at his feet, then at Sleepy and then back at the floor.

"Well, I guess that's it," Sleepy said. "Jimmy and Bull will sit this game out. Now for the rest of you..."

"Wait, wait," Jonesy spoke up, "it wasn't their fault. They were just trying to help my..."

"Stop," Sleepy forcefully interrupted. "Jonesy, if Jimmy and Bull can't stand in front of me and explain their actions then it's their problem, not yours. Now I know you feel bad that your buddies can't play, but that's the way it's going to be." Jonesy tried to speak again, but Sleepy turned his back, but before he left he turned back towards the team and said, "Just because Bull and Jimmy aren't playing doesn't mean we can't win." He then opened the door and walked out.

The room was silent until Jimmy spoke. "You know, coach is right. Just because Bull and I aren't playing doesn't mean we can't win. Everybody in this room has been sweating and working hard all year. Coach has taught us to play as a team and we've been doing it. Jonesy, you can keep us in the game with your shooting. Too Tall, when you lose yourself in the game there isn't a better center. Tommy, you're the quickest guard in this tournament." Jimmy went on giving everyone in the room an emotional lift.

Jimmy was feeling the emotion of a whole season welling up inside of him. He regretted not being able to play, but he wasn't going to let his teammates down again. "Listen guys, Bull and I are going to be on the sideline going crazy. We'll be cheering and losing ourselves in the game. I know we can do it if we pull together and play as a team. We have to believe we can win." With that the guys huddled together, clasped hands and stayed silent for a few moments. When they headed out to the floor they had the look of determination usually associated with men twice their age.

The sounds of the bands and the cheers of the cheerleaders filled the Arena as the Eagles ran onto the floor. The fans were ready to see if the storybook Carver High Eagles could finish their improbable season.

The number-one-rated Chamberlain Bearcats were already shooting lay-ups as the Eagles took the floor. The Eagles broke into two lines to do their lay-up drills when the crowd suddenly realized that Jimmy and Bull weren't dressed to play. A quiet buzz swept over the stands.

———————

Ted knew he had had a close call last night. Pretty soon he was going to get caught by the police or somebody like Pepper Brown was going to hurt him. As soon as Ted got into his car he turned his radio to the station carrying the game. Then he heard the announcers say that Jimmy and Bull were not dressed for the game.

Ted knew it was his fault. He had asked them to help and this is what they got in return. Ted had never had a lower opinion of himself than he did now. He knew his dealing and drug use was ruining his whole life. Now he had even gotten his brother's friends involved.

Ted knew he had to do something. His brother had been so excited about the basketball season and now he had screwed everything up. He had to change everything in his life. He had to change or his brother would never respect him again. An idea hit Ted like a thunderbolt. He knew exactly what he had to do.

———————

Skits could barely concentrate on the game. The conversation that he had had with Sleepy this morning was still fresh in his mind. The greatest basketball player of all time had tempted him with an exclusive story. Skits needed to know what Sleepy was up to. "Maybe he's going to coach in the NBA," Skits thought. Skits knew that if he had an exclusive on that story it would be the biggest scoop of his career. Skits didn't even notice when the buzzer sounded to start the game.

The buzzer woke Sleepy from a foggy daydream. He had been reliving the moment when he lost the bet with Jimmy at the golf course and had gotten himself into all of this. He thought about the season and the good relationship he had developed with these young men. It was too bad that it had to end this way. Sleepy chided himself for losing his focus. He knew he needed to practice what he preached and lose himself in the game. He quickly righted himself and called the boys into a huddle in front of the bench.

Mrs. Feen was sitting with the rest of the parents in the reserved section of the bleachers. She was surprised to see her son standing behind the huddle without his uniform on. "What's the matter with Jimmy?" she asked Kim, who was sitting next to her.

"I don't know," Kim answered. She was just as surprised as everyone else.

Sleepy looked around at all of his players. He could see that they were ready to give it their all. "As you know, this is the number-one-rated team in the tournament. I know we're missing Bull and Jimmy, but if you try hard, sweat hard and push yourselves, we can win. I know we can." Sleepy's voice was getting emotional and the team was feeding off that emotion. "We have to play as a team," Sleepy continued. "Call out picks, pass the ball and pick away. Play the game, play it as a team and we can win this thing. Now everybody in." When it came time to scream "GO EAGLES", Jimmy and Bull screamed the loudest.

"One last thing," Sleepy said. "Willie and Mark start for Jimmy and Bull."

"Come on guys, you can do it," Jimmy encouraged his teammates as they took the floor. Jimmy knew that his team was overmatched, but he wasn't going to sulk. He was willing to do anything, even the slightest thing, to help his team win. Sleepy looked at Jimmy and couldn't help but feel proud of this young man. Even though he was mad at Jimmy, he admired his positive attitude.

Too Tall won the tip and the Eagles ran a perfect tip play with Mark cutting to the ball and then hitting Kenny under the basket for an easy lay-up. The Eagles were pumped up and their full-court defense forced three quick turnovers. The Eagles converted all three into baskets and jumped to an 8-0 lead. The Chamberlain coach then called for a timeout.

After the timeout, the slow, methodical Chamberlain team began to exploit the Eagles' weaknesses. By the end of the first quarter Chamberlain's superior strength and quickness had enabled them to pull ahead by one point, 13-12.

Ted knew that he couldn't change all of the bad things he had done, but he could explain to Sleepy Phillips exactly what had happened. Ted parked his car in the Arena's large parking lot and then headed toward the nearest ticket counter.

"We're all sold out today," the ticket lady said to Ted as he approached.

"I have a ticket waiting for me." Ted explained that his brother played on the team.

The lady looked his name up on the computer and then smiled as she gave Ted his ticket. "Have a nice time," she told him. Ted rushed in through the gate and felt a wave of excitement as he leaned over the balcony and saw the brilliant colors of a basketball game below. Ted stopped only long enough to see his brother out on the floor and then he headed for the locker room.

Had Ted stopped long enough to watch the game, he would have seen an unbelievable second quarter performance. Jimmy, Bull and Jonesy would talk about this quarter for the rest of their lives. Jonesy was on fire. He wasn't playing for himself or his brother, he was playing for his two best friends. He wanted to repay Jimmy and Bull by losing himself in the game. He knew his two friends had risked their own welfare to help his family. A guy couldn't have two better friends, he knew.

Jonesy put his mind to the task at hand and played harder than he had ever known he could play. He dove after loose balls, played aggressive, demanding defense and worked himself free for open jump shots. These jump shots were the only thing keeping the Eagles reasonably close. Jonesy took 10 shots in the second quarter and made nine. It was a shooting display a professional would have been proud of. Despite these heroics, Chamberlain took a commanding 45-30 lead into halftime.

Ted made his way to the locker room door and once he did, he realized that he had no chance to sneak by the security. It was too tight, but he had to explain the situation to Sleepy. He had to find some way.

The second half began much the same way as the first ended, with Chamberlain working the ball inside for easy lay-ups or foul shots. Even though the Eagles came out of the locker room fired up and played inspired basketball, Chamberlain had too much for the undermanned Eagles. As Chamberlain built a twenty-point lead, Sleepy began to think about what he was going to say to his team after the game. It had been a wonderful season for him and he wanted to thank the boys for all of their hard work.

One thing kept bothering Sleepy as he sat on the bench, however. Why in the world wouldn't Jimmy tell him what had happened. The police had said something about Bull and Jimmy trying to help someone. Sleepy just wished they had told him what had happened.

Ted saw his opening. Even though he would have to disrupt the whole game, he knew he had to do it. As the last seconds ticked off the clock for the third quarter, Jonesy hit a three-pointer to close the gap to seventeen points. The buzzer sounded as the ball went through the hoop. Jonesy turned back to the bench only to see his brother run past him and toward Sleepy.

Ted sprinted straight for Sleepy, who was still sitting on the bench. Security guards hired to protect Sleepy stormed the floor and grabbed Ted, but Jimmy, Bull and Jonesy raced to the now swelling group of people around Sleepy and Ted.

"Don't hurt him. He's my brother," Jonesy screamed, but the noise was so loud nobody heard him. Jimmy finally wiggled his way in between everyone and grabbed his coach.

"That's Jonesy's brother. He's not crazy or anything, so can you tell the bodyguards to let him go?" Jimmy asked. Sleepy told his security guards to let Ted go and they did.

"If he isn't crazy then why is he running out in the middle of the court?" Sleepy asked. Ted was now standing right in front of Sleepy with security guards, tournament officials, players, and police standing all around. Mrs. Feen could see everything clearly from her vantage point, although like the rest of the crowd, she had no idea what was going on.

"Mr. Phillips," Ted said nervously, "I'm sorry I had to make such a big scene like this, but it was the only way I could talk to you before the game ended. The reason I'm standing here is to tell you why Jimmy and Bull were at the police station last night." Ted was shaking noticeably, but his younger brother was listening proudly. Jonesy knew that his older brother would do the right thing. He had just known it.

"I called Jimmy and asked for his help," Ted continued. "I'm not proud to say it, but I've been messing around with drugs and I owed a bad dude some money. I didn't want my little brother to know, so I asked Jimmy. All Jimmy was doing last night was bringing me the money so I wouldn't get hurt. I know Jimmy didn't tell you any of this because he's that kind of guy. He probably wanted to protect my name, for whatever reason." As Ted said this his face dropped and

Sleepy could tell that the young man was now fully realizing the trouble he had gotten himself into.

Sleepy looked at Jimmy. He couldn't help but to be a little mad at himself for not being more understanding. This boy was helping out another and got caught in a bad situation. "How did Bull get mixed up in this," Sleepy asked, remembering Bull was also at the police station.

"Let me answer that one," Jonesy said as he stepped into the middle of the group. "Bull found out that Jimmy was going and insisted on going with him. He didn't want Jimmy going alone." Again, Sleepy felt a wave of guilt. These two long-time friends were top-notch boys.

"I hate to jump in the middle of this," a referee said as he blew his whistle, "but we have a game to finish."

"Yes we do," Sleepy said as he turned to Jimmy and Bull, who were standing there in plain clothes. "I don't want to get all sentimental, but I wish you had told me this." Jimmy and Bull were both anxiously looking at the ground. Sleepy then realized they were itching to get into the game. He looked at Jimmy and Bull and said sternly, "Get into the locker room and get dressed. Your uniforms are in the equipment bag." Before any of this had sunk in to the other players, Jimmy and Bull were sprinting towards the locker room.

The referees finally removed everyone from the court and started the fourth quarter of play. Jimmy and Bull made their way back to the bench with just over seven minutes to play and Chamberlain ahead by sixteen points. As soon as they appeared, Sleepy inserted them into the game and they made an immediate difference. Jimmy stole the ball twice and scored easy lay-ups. The Eagles then used their full-court press to make another steal. Jonesy quickly passed the ball to Jimmy in the middle of the court. Jimmy drove down the lane and then finished with a mighty slam dunk and the crowd exploded.

The momentum swing of the 6-0 run wasn't lost on Chamberlain's coach who called an immediate timeout. He was determined not to let this game get away from his team. On the opposite end of the court, Sleepy was just as determined to give his team a chance to win.

"Good job, fellas," Sleepy said excitedly. "We're only ten points down with four minutes left. We can do it." With that the boys took the floor and resumed their all-out press. Chamberlain was a disciplined team and their coach had settled them down during the timeout. Now, instead of trying to score, they were trying to milk the clock and shorten the game.

Bull was muscling the opposing guards on defense and was called for a foul. The opponent missed the free throw and Too Tall grabbed the rebound and passed it to Jimmy at mid-court. Jimmy dribbled straight for a defensive player. He stopped in front of the defensive man and dribbled the ball back and forth across his shoe tops. The defender took the bait and tried to steal the ball, allowing Jimmy to easily slide by him. Kenny was motioning for the ball in the corner and Jimmy hit him with a forceful chest pass.

What happened next can't be practiced or rehearsed. It just comes instinctively. Jimmy continued his run down the center of the court. Kenny saw this and gave him a return pass, but the ball floated high and towards the rim. Jimmy raced after it, jumped and grabbed the ball in mid-air and then stuffed it in the basket. The crowd again erupted with a roar that resonated to the rafters. The Eagles were now behind by only eight points with two minutes to play.

Chamberlain stayed with its strategy of stalling. With 1:29 left to play, Jimmy fouled Chamberlain's big center. He missed the foul shot and Bull rebounded. The Eagles quickly worked the ball to the other end. Kenny whipped the ball to Bull in the corner. Bull faked inside to Too Tall and flipped a cross-court pass to Jonesy over Chamberlain's zone defense. Jonesy set up for a shot, but passed to Jimmy as the defense converged on him. Jimmy, without hesitation, went up for his shot, well beyond the three-point line. Nothing but net. The Eagles now trailed by only five with a little less than a minute to go.

Chamberlain's coach was yelling for his players to call a timeout, but they couldn't hear him over the roar of the crowd. Bull rushed towards the point guard as he received the inbounds pass. The point guard was tired and hurried a pass up the floor. Jimmy had been watching the point guard's movements from the half-court line and saw him begin to pass the ball. Jimmy, with fresh legs, stepped in front of the Chamberlain player and easily made the steal.

Jimmy saw an opening down the center of the floor and took it. He dribbled hard to the foul line and in one fluid motion, faked a pass to Jonesy in the corner and continued toward the basket with the ball held in his right hand, high over his head. Jimmy swooped in towards the basket and as he rose high above the rim, he windmill dunked the ball. The crowd went insane.

The Eagles were now down three points with thirty-four seconds left. Jimmy headed back down the court after dunking the ball, but out of the corner of his eye he could see Chamberlain's point guard. The point guard was waiting for the inbounds pass. Jimmy waited one more moment and then he turned suddenly, hoping the pass was on its way. It was. Like a laser streak, Jimmy stole the ball and laid it in the basket, cutting the lead to a single point.

Chamberlain's coach finally called his team's last timeout. Sleepy rushed his players to the bench. "All right guys, great pressure. We only need two more points to win this game." Sleepy paused and looked at the clock. "As soon as the other team gets the ball in, foul whoever has the ball. If they miss the foul shot all we need is a two-point basket for the win. If they make both foul shots we need a three pointer to tie." Sleepy then set up a play to run. Kenny was to take the ball up the court and look for Jimmy on the sideline. Too Tall and Bull were to pick off Jimmy's defensive man, freeing him for a shot. If Jimmy wasn't open or couldn't get his shot off, Jonesy was to free himself in the corner for a jump shot as the last option.

The buzzer rang calling the players back out onto the court. The Eagles quickly fouled Chamberlain's point guard. He missed the first shot and Kenny came down with the long rebound. Kenny hurried the ball up the floor and waited as Jimmy ran along the baseline. Too Tall and Bull tried to pick off his man, but Chamberlain had prepared during the timeout and had two players guarding Jimmy.

Kenny tried to force the ball to Jimmy in the corner. One of the defensive players deflected the pass, but Jimmy ran to it and took control. He was standing twenty-five feet away from the basket with the clock down to five seconds. Two men were in defensive positions directly in front of him. Jimmy started to dribble and faked like he was going left and then faked back to his right. The defensive players stayed put. Jimmy, realizing he had no time to do anything else, jumped and shot the ball. The game buzzer sounded as the ball rose high above the basket.

The coaches, the players, the fans and even the security guards stopped and watched as the ball began its downward arc. The Arena was deadly silent. The shot felt good to Jimmy as it left his hand. The ball fell towards the basket, but hit the back of the rim. It bounced around the rim and then went straight up, before falling back towards the basket. It seemed to everyone in the Arena that the ball was moving in slow motion. The ball hit the rim again and fell off to the side.

Jimmy stood in crushed disbelief as the Chamberlain players celebrated around him. They were jumping up and down and hugging each other. Jimmy lingered around the court for awhile and then, finally, he trudged to the locker room with the rest of his teammates.

CHAPTER XVII

The Conclusion

Skits did as Sleepy had asked. He didn't print the reason why Bull and Jimmy had sat out the first three quarters. He mentioned that it was a coaching decision and left it at that. Everyone in St. Louis wanted to know why Jimmy and Bull didn't play the first three quarters and who had run onto the floor, but they never got an answer. Skits did this because he wanted the big story that Sleepy had tempted him with. However, Skits also knew he didn't print the truth because of his growing affection for the players and Jimmy in particular.

Sleepy did come through for Skits with the big story. He announced on a nationally-televised interview with Skits that he was going to come out of retirement and play again in the NBA. Sleepy said that the season with the ninth graders had shown him how much he loved the game and missed the competition.

Just as Sleepy had predicted, the fans quickly forgot about the Carver Eagles once baseball season started. One person that didn't forget however, was Mrs. Feen. She was curious as to why her son didn't play the first three quarters of the championship game, but she never asked him. She had raised her son right and she knew that he could make his own way, although she was still curious.

Ted's decision to interrupt the game was the best decision of his life. He and Jonesy started a new relationship, one in which they talked openly about their problems and their dreams.

Kim knew for sure that Jimmy Feen was the man for her, but she didn't press him to actually say they were boyfriend and girlfriend. She hoped someday that he would decide this for himself.

As for Jimmy Feen and Sleepy Phillips, Jimmy received his report card and it read all A's and B's. He had won the bet. Jimmy didn't know that Sleepy had called and talked to his mother shortly after the Eagles' season had ended. They set up a surprise for Jimmy.

One night when Jimmy, Bull and the rest of the gang were playing at their neighborhood courts, Sleepy unexpectedly showed up to pay off on his bet. The older guys at the court were awestruck by the sight of him and Sleepy showed them what the greatest basketball player of all time could really do. Jimmy especially liked the fact that the first shot Sleepy tried was a thunderous dunk right on top of big Lucius Jackson.

Lucius glared at Jimmy and his friends as they doubled over in laughter. When the night was over, Sleepy shook hands with everyone and signed a few autographs.

"I'm not betting you anymore," Sleepy said to Jimmy as he got in his car at the end of the night.

"We'll see about that," Jimmy replied with a big smile.

After Sleepy had left, Jimmy, Bull, Jonesy, Kenny and the rest of the gang headed home. They talked about girls, school, basketball and, of course, Sleepy Phillips.

— The End —